To order paperback or eBook copies of ***Clones and Angels*** go to Amazon.com and to Kindle.

jchesterrobertson@gmail.com

Robertson, John Chester

Clones and Angels/ John Chester Robertson

ISBN 978-1-7322684-5-6

1st Edition

Dedications

Courtney T. Dorsey

Connor R. Dorsey

Delanie R. Robertson

Lauren O. Robertson

Prolog

Most of the world believes in one or more spirits. We call them by various names. Clones and Angels and the preceding novel, Vigilante Spirit, imagines a place between heaven, hell and wherever else. Especially at those existing and working in a dimension mortals cannot see.

Mortals and immortals share common problems. Both fall from comfortable and even exalted pedestals. Then we try to regain our lost position. A few succeed in climbing back up. Sadly, most are worse off than ever. There is always hope.

Science and faith enlighten the area between where we exist and other beings each in different language. Still both strive to explain the space. In Vigilante Spirit we explain our concept. Clones and Angels expands in an entertaining way. Is the unseen supernatural simply another dimension of nature? Perhaps it is, but definitely out of sight. Please decide for yourself.

– Jack Robertson

CONTENTS

1

HUNTER

People have believed in something beyond life and death since the beginning when man first looked up to the stars. Those fortunate enough to believe in heaven and hell usually are stuck with the question of what's in between And where those charged with carrying out the divine exist and how they behave. We have a logical way of seeing this though the eyes of our immortals.

Lucien and her new husband are guardian angels. Prior to their recent wedding he was an echo spirit known as Vigilante. While everything he achieved as a spirit was with the best intentions, they agree tweaks are needed for those deeds to be worthy of the angel he became when they married.

These lovers scheme to ensure righteousness. Starting with poor dead Hunter. A lad who was slain because he was mistaken for his dead father who in life was a coldhearted robber. Hunter was mistaken for his father and shot dead in the town of Buzzardville by its' nearsighted sheriff.

Hunter lies stiff and cold in his grave. Morning never dawns beneath the surface of this ground for these resting in the chapel cemetery. For everyone buried here in this haunted abode, it's always as cold and dark as night. Ghosts entombed beneath this sanctified sod lie immobile consumed by their longings and fears. For just this one lucky youth, his internment is nearly over.

Here lies Hunter who was promised escape. This lad has faith his miserable state of limbo will soon have passed. *"How or when?"* *"Does my being saved mean I'm going to heaven?"* One thing he does knows is- *"I'm horribly cold..."* Waiting is unbearable. But what else is there for the dead?

Laying here for the first time, Hunter regrets his mistakes in judgement that led him to be murdered. *"If I just knew..."* From other tombstones the phrase echoes, *"If only..."* Moans another, *"This freaking ground is freezin'!"*

Events that brought his frigid being to this end happened entirely too fast for Hunter's slow mind. Still he wouldn't acknowledge the voice inside of his head. One that tried to warn him, screaming, *"Hunter don't take the loot to Buzzardville."* It was stashed just yards from this grave. It is now back in the hands of its' rightful owners.

Hunter wails to himself, *"Once I had a cabin, a hunting dog, and more ducks and fish than anyone could hope for...."* *"Then BANG!"* *"Without warning, everything changed!"* Laying here now in a makeshift wooden coffin, it's become extremely obvious he shouldn't have taken the loot his father hid under the old alter stone.

His first mistake was he assumed he inherited even the stolen things his father left behind just as he inherited the cabin. His fathers' mortal remains lay nearby. Hunter actually dug that grave. Father is just beneath another dirt mound mere yards away where Hunter buried him when he died. There was no one else to bury him but a son who also inherited his curse.

Neither has tried to communicate with one another

because Hunter's coffin was dropped below these weeds barely a week ago. And, neither ever will speak to the other again. Instantly the old mans' wretched soul was carried away to its' ultimate misery by the grim reaper. The explanation, *"Your cursed soul shan't stain this sanctified ground."* This was one of his easier selections.

"He's down in hells' pit; it was a slam dunk!", remarked *Gee*, a nickname his friends have tagged on heaven and hells' infamous angel of death. Gee is well known in all dimensions as the dreaded grim reaper. *Hells' pit* is the deepest most foul destination of agony, a place far lower than the reach of cellphone and Wi-Fi. Only after being killed by mistake in nearby Buzzardville and buried here in that rough wooden crate has Hunter fully come to understand his father's curse. His second chance was the gift of angels. He blew his first chance; it was the bequest of demons.

Except for those decent folks whose property was stolen, this curse destroys everyone connected to that plunder. His father was the robber the curse was destined to destroy. It then transferred to that robbers' son. From the black sky above, the curse against Hunter is about to be erased. The earth begins to tremble.

A beastly rumble belches from within the belly of the darkest shadow far above this worldly hellhole. With precise aim, a brilliant flash of lightning slams arcs downward to where Hunter lay. It hits the base of his coffin. Hunter feels the rough box upend amidst a shower of splinters. His electrified corpse is shocked upright. Briskly the sensation of pain returns to him. His cracked lips barely mutter, *"One inch higher and I'd be burnt toast!"*

A faint tingling in his toes then a twitching of his nose. He senses. *"I'm alive!"* He sense something else, a familiar pounding, *"I feel my heart beating!"* The nails holding the makeshift coffin boards to make the box melt like birthday candles in the lightnings' heat. His arm flies up to protect his face; the coffin lid bursts off. He jolts upright.

Cautiously he peeks out, then pokes his right foot out into the rain, then the left. His body reluctantly follows his feet.

He is vertical This is the first moment since being shot. Looking out and down is a great luxury to a corpse. Although his cold body is ridged and stiff he can move his legs. He doesn't even mind the twinge in one from an old dog bite.

Still shivering, he screams, *"It's great to be real again!"* Hunter peers around the rainy moldy churchyard. He cries out- *"What a beautiful day to be alive!"*

With determination, he makes his way to the chapel stumbling over slippery rocks. Once out of the heavy downpour he stands before the same rustic altar he by his greed desecrated.. *"Alas Lord, I am so much wiser for wear."* With his head humbly bent, Hunter whispers the wonderful nearly forgotten psalm his mother once read to her family-

> *"The LORD is my shepherd; I shall not want.*
> *He maketh me to lie down in green pastures:*
> *He leadeth me beside the still waters.*
> *He restoreth my soul ...."*

After this prayer of thanks to the Almighty, Hunter meanders down towards his old cabin by the swamp. Ghostly graveyard thinkers measure in wonder his every step. *"What manner of creature is this?"*

He will change his bloody clothes and cleanse himself as best he can; then walk to town. The way to Grace is simple. Just follow the old road. Hunter has faith it will faithfully lead him to his mother and brother. His one wish: to find them.

He returns to the road passing the border of the churchyard. Its' ghostly inhabitants are always there. Their incessant chatter is no longer heard by his ears. Their total silence is proof to Hunter he's alive again. Yet within the limits of this hidden dimension these graveyard denizens are bobbing their bones up and down in sheer joy. *"One of us got away!"*

They debate among themselves is whether Hunter is really alive or if he's just another zombie? Although he can no longer hear those graveyard ghosts, he sympathizes with their confusion. He makes a noisy show of gathering and consuming blackberries and nuts along his way.

He wants to make his *being alive* status obvious to them. A gloomy soul observes, *"No zombie is stupid enough to stroll through sticker bushes the way he just did!"* Hunter's painful scratches prove to himself he is alive. He realizes he just proven to them and himself by walking though the thorny bushes. One sums it up for the graveyard crew, *"He's alive but nuts!"*

Once back within his musty cabin, Hunter finds his rusty razor he stashed within the versatile chamber pot. He squints into a cracked mirror attacking his unkempt beard. Once again cleanshaven he is happy. Aside from an extremely pasty facial pallor, he doesn't seem to be someone who has just returned from the grave.

The clothes he's wearing are covered with dried blood, splinters, and cemetery dirt. He gathers up what's left of his wardrobe and finds somewhat better clothes; then tosses the ones he wore into the fireplace. He feels slightly warmer and much more human. Revived now, Hunter heads towards Buzzardville clutching blackberries and nuts slung in a rag sack over one shoulder.

An unearthly shriek in the hidden dimension, Hunter still can't hear is the only sign his benefactors are watching. The angel known in the past as Vigilante says to wife Lucien, *"Hunter can't follow the same path!" "He'll be shot all over again just as soon as he walks into Buzzardville!"* She cracks up laughing and looks him in the eye. Reading her mind, he grasps the sheer insanity about to happen.

A long black limo pulls up alongside of Hunter as he walks once again down the road to death. The chauffer in black uniform speaks to him, *"Young man, I believe your mothers' name is Grace." "Is that correct?"* Hunter affirms excitedly, *"Yes, do you know where my mother lives?"*

The driver stops the limo and steps out replying, *"I'm Morris, Ms. Grace asked me to bring you home to her.."* Holding the door open to the rear seats, he says, *"Please step in and we will soon be with Ms. Grace and your brother Malcolm."*

This is the first time he's heard Mal's full first name in years, if ever. After the enormous jolt he got this morning nothing surprises Hunter. So he doesn't bother to ask Morris how Grace could know he's trying to find her.

Morris navigates the big fast limo the most roundabout way imaginable to avoid passing through Buzzardville. Morris understands the danger very well. Sheriff McPherson's town is not on their itinerary. He steps on the throttle; they pick up speed. Hunter feels more alive now than ever. So alive and hungry that he eats all of his berries.

He was in such a hurry to leave the cabin Hunter forgot to put out the fire he started to warm himself. The cold bottomless chill felt beneath the ground was severe. Even though his heart resumed sending warm blood through his body. Even after warming up, the boneyard cold is still making him shiver. He barely remembers it because he's so excited. But for the same reason when he walked out of the cabin Hunter didn't notice something else.

A heavy drooping branch had overgrown and nearly covered the cabin chimney. Although its' leaves were greenish yellow when he opened the chimney damper, they turned brown as the blaze caught on.

Soon they dried completely from smoke rising up the chimney. Like the tinder they were, the leaves burned. A slight breeze feeds a burning cinder. The dry leaf clusters flare up. Connecting twigs ignite the entire branch.

Soft orange flames turn light red then dark blue. Searing flames bore through the cabin roof and down its' sides lighting up the ancient logs like so many matchsticks. The cabin is doomed. The limo is barely out of sight when the cabin's old pine roof blew up in flame. Morris sees it in his rear view mirror but doesn't tell his passenger.

Although he can't see his cabin burn, Hunter has no home here to return to ever. He is homeless unless he finds Grace and Mal …assuming they allow him to live with them. Morris sets his jaw determined to avoid the town and to get Hunter to his mother.

Another creature was much closer to the cabin fire though. As Hunter came into the cabin, a polecat, descended from the infamous Polecat Puppy, scurried beneath the bed. Sensing the smoke, it managed to beat paws through the door and outside just in time to avoid becoming a roasted polecat. It retreated to its' hiding place beneath the outhouse.

For Hunter. just being alive again is astounding and leaving his cabin is unimportant. However, he was born and raised in that burned down cabin. The only reason he left it for Buzzardville where he was murdered is because a meddling spirit infused this lad and his dog with a great deal more intellect than they had before he found them. *"They're too damned smart now for their own good,"* said one cranky angel.

Vigilante's form has evolved greatly since then. No longer a mere spirit, he has new responsibilities. Resolving gaffes made as a spirit, when it is possible, he will improve toxic outcomes. Hunter is just one of several situations he wants to improve.

"Let's talk about you." Lucien is firm. But her husband doesn't really want more huge changes in his existence. *"Just being married to you is good enough for*

me…" But it isn't for her. So, like most former bachelors, he realizes he must change for the two to be compatible. They settle down in an empty room. She begins by explaining, *"A third millennium angel is unlike any of the past…"* He rolls his eyes and pretends to go to sleep declaring, *"Bull feathers!"*

"People and God still have the same relationship." She patiently continues on, *"People now have it so easy they think it all just happens." "Too much spare time gets human beings in trouble." "They hurt one another often for no reason other than boredom."*

He senses she has something in mind and doesn't roll his eyes again. Still maintaining his dignity, he won't ask her questions until later. And she will let solving the worlds' problems pass for now. But this dialog persists day after day. He stops wondering why and reality dawns on him- *"Lucien is teaching me knowledge a guardian angel must have."*

Appreciating his intuition she smiles; he senses she has just informed him very diplomatically to recognize his innate ignorance. Not wishing to be as stupid as he feels at this moment he decides to listen without being disagreeable. Not a moment too soon for Lucien as she was losing her patience.

He smiles at her- *"You are the light of my existence!"* Lucien covers her puckered lips with one wing and blows him a kiss. He is floored because his passion for this beautiful angel has overwhelmed him since the first moment he saw her as they joined their talents to save a young innocent girl. That girl is now Angela. Lucien is her guardian angel.

Angela's life was troubled from the instant she was born to an evil wretch after a one night affair with the late Will Gold. It was fantastically improved when mysteriously she became recognized as the beautiful daughter of the reclusive billionaire. In her past Angela was so vulnerable that she will always be the target of evil. Although she doesn't remember anything of her wretched past, her guardian angel remembers and will always be on her side. Lucien is her most powerful supporter.

2

PRISTINE

An echo spirit and an angel married during a boisterous ceremony at a 18th century red brick chapel on the eastern shore. Despite serious attempts by demonic forces, and even another spurned angel, nuptials were completed. Then this newly appointed angel took the hand of his beloved angel Lucien.

As an echo spirit he was Vigilante Spirit. This name is inappropriate for an angel. Lucien suddenly wants her new husband to decide upon a dignified name as an angel. But as her rejected suitor puts it, *"Lucien is no ordinary angel!"*

There was serious deception on the part of his bride. Jealous suiter Roman objected to their marriage and unveiled her true identity. He revealed Lucien to be the very angel who Vigilante thought he was rebounding from. His solution was to marry Mercy a similar and more compatible echo spirit. It didn't work; he loves Lucien more than ever instantly forgiving her deceptions.

Only within this bizarre dimension, could any love be so strange and beautiful. He is so in love as to forgive Lucien's' devious disguise. Even after he took her to the altar believing Lucien to be Mercy, a spirit. He thought Mercy was also a spirit rather than Lucien, a beautiful angel. This is a dimension where spirits, angels and demons exist completely hidden from our conscious view. He doesn't dare to think about how it would have worked out if Roman hadn't revealed her identity as the nuptials began.

The problem of where his education to become a professional guardian angel can take place is indirectly solved by Roman. Although he is her rebuffed suitor, Roman now accepts being rejected by Lucien. Graciously he entrusts Hiker, an ostensibly settled human client, to this neophyte angel. Roman suggests to everyone he is going away for substance abuse. But really, Roman's new mission is to evaluate a worthy candidate to receive his services as a guardian angel. It is believable because Roman's problem happens to be true. He is addicted to sniffing beer bubbles... and anything else aromatic he can get his nose into from honeysuckle flowers to moonshine.

For any creatures of the hidden dimension, who've been around Roman when he's intoxicated, this is a plausible reason to seek treatment. However, Roman is using it as a cover to prevent fallen angels from swarming in if the candidate for guardian angel is not quite suitable. Spirits and immortals exist in an element where the good and the evil too easily observe the actions of one another. Lucien finds it amusing.

She chuckles, *"Try to imagine an AA meeting with invisible Roman's voice booming, "My name is Roman." "Because I sniff beer bubbles!" "I am a sniff-oholic!"*

Lucien, her new husband, and Roman would have been a hoot rather than a haunt living together in the same house after the wedding. Roman disliked Lucien's new husband before the ceremony and actually convinced Vigilante that Lucian didn't love him when they were going together. Rather than fight with Roman, Lucien made an end-run on her true love almost breaking his heart all of their way to the altar.

To Roman's credit, he's doing the best he can by staying away from them now. Secretly Roman believes both have such strong egos their love will fly off in opposite directions. Angela knows what he's up to and tells her husband. He assures her, *"I'm not going anywhere."*

Both celestial and mortal couples currently reside in the big house on the hill along with a dog. This almost but not quite heroic animal is a retriever. His name is either *Dog* or *Dumb ass,* depending on who you ask. It doesn't matter, he never comes when anyone calls him anyway.

As for visitors, occasionally a few stray ghosts show up unexpectedly. They ignore the canine and the couples. Ghosts do their own thing. Dog thinks they're cool. All dwell within the big old house Angela inherited from her father.

Almost by coincidence, neither Angela nor Lucien's relationship with their husbands has been altogether transparent. In Lucien's case, she always knew she charmed him from the moment they met. Once Lucien saw him for the good spirit he was, she fell in love with him. He adored her from the first moment their paths crossed. But he still doesn't have a name.

He simply accepts each nuance of her personality she reveals without complaint and keeps coming back for more. More is about to come. For instance, he still thinks she's a simple everyday guardian angel. Even though her name Lucien doesn't exactly fit the classic guardian angel profile. *"I don't care!"* is what he says to himself whenever negative thoughts come to mind. He's come a long way; he likes having a body. It greatly improves their marital relationship.

Of the resident mortals, neither Angela nor her husband hiker are aware her face was reconstructed. Or that she grew up in far less savory circumstance with her witch of a mother. Not just her face, her body was also surgically restored. Both required major surgery because a demonic thug known as the Strangler hurt her so badly. If Hiker knew she was reconstructed, he wouldn't care, He only loves the beautiful Angela he knows. There's a lot of love in the big house on the hill.

Strangler's soul, echo spirit and its' splinter have all been exorcised. But Strangler didn't go down easily.

Hopefully, Strangler and every last shred of his being are down in hell where they can't hurt anyone. Gee acknowledges. *"Unfortunately, the world is full of demonic mortals who are just as bad."*

Angel Lucien, whose name suggests *enlightener,* will gradually reveal her hidden nature over time as her husband understands her better. He is learning as her student and her beloved. And, as was Raven to a significant degree he is her subordinate. She never expresses this thought. Reading her husbands' thoughts and expression she smiles disarmingly explaining, *"We modern angels multitask!"*

As for Raven: at a critical moment for Angela's father, Raven was seduced by a demon posing as a crow. Raven's distraction at the very instant Will Gold was about to die set this entire epic in motion. This is good because no one could make these events up. And Lucien's mate still doesn't have a name.

For the angels, there are many problems coming to challenge them. Just one for example, human clones are being smuggled into their very neighborhood. Three of these will have a disturbing effect on their tranquility. Angela is aware of them but feels angels may not noticeably interfere. It is up to humans to survive trials thrown at them. How other to determine their worth in the eternal paradigm? Even so, she can watch and when possible offer subliminal advice. She smiles, *"That's what guardian angels are for." "We're sneaky!"*

Her husband sees these clones as intruders. Adversaries he may decide to destroy. Lucien listens but says nothing. They have no idea just how close the clone problem is going to come to the big house. Lucien rationalizes, *"At least no one can clone angels."* He husband reads her mind, smiles, and says, *"If we could I'd clone you."* She smiles, *"Have you seen yourself in a mirror since you became an angel?"* She adds, *"And you certainly need a name."* He stammers; she interrupts, *"Don't argue, Go look in the mirror and think of a name for yourself!"* He's never had a reason to look into a mirror because he didn't have a body. He looks into the mirror in the hall and sees absolutely nothing. Lucien hands him her mirror.

He sees his angel body for the first time. After way too much self-love his wife snatches back her mirror. *"You are conceited!"* she screams. He purposely smiles at her for the first time.

3

A NAME

At this point, Lucien's nameless husband is much more than a barely real echo spirit. He asserts, *"My values haven't changed one bit!"* Sticking to his guns he asserts his ethic to her, *"Protection of innocence is the key element of who I am Lucien; I maintain a passion for justice beyond my duties as a guardian. I can't deny who I am any more than I can deny my love for you."* This part of his independence declaration softens her resistance. She touches his hand.

Dedication to righteousness was a major factor in why he triumphed in his quest to be with her. Dog and Raven are taking this discussion in; Raven is puzzled. Dog explains it to Raven very simply, *"He chased Lucien 'til that sly ole Lucien caught him."* Raven just flutters her wings thinking, *"I'll be glad when I'm out of here."*

Before his elevation to angel, it would have been unseemly for a high-ranking guardian angel to court a humble ephemeral spirit. To appear to be on an equal plane with him she took the shape of an echo spirit.

As a guardian angel, Lucien expects him to assume a gentle angelic persona. She is resolute, *"It begins with your new name." "You are now a member of a highly organized social group;" "You are no longer an island of one."*

She pleads with him, *"Decide on your new name as an angel."* He absorbs all of this except her demand that he pick his new name. Nothing in his past experience gives him any inkling, He asks, *"How do I pick a name?"*

She hasn't experienced this problem either and needs time to think. Instead of answering, Lucien lectures, her husband, to be less spontaneous and more thoughtful. *"At the first sign of a bad situation an angel doesn't just charge into battle."* It's the sad lot of all guardian angels, *"Human events for better or worse must be allowed to unfold naturally."* Though for the moment he seems settled, she remembers his hot impulsive nature and doesn't want it to erupt.

He stews over the problem. To accommodate Lucien he chooses a gentlemanly name. *"Just call me Ralph."* The name suits Lucien as it is one derived from an acceptable guardian angel tradition. He doesn't realize his name will actually be listed in the celestial logbook as Raphael.

Although he doesn't realize it, officially Raphael has just decided to call himself *Ralph*. But will the ghosts and spirits accept him by this rather unusual name? The opinion of demons and devils don't matter. She giggles thinking of the surprise he has in store. Ralph thinks she's overjoyed with his choice. Lucien puts it out of her mind.

His accomplishment as the spirit who saved Clyde, the forsaken ghost of sunken Oriole Island, has this "Ralph" already regarded a hero to the ghosts of the Patapsco valley. Ghosts who haunt this stream are thrilled to have this great guy in their neighborhood and are happy to call him Vigilante, Ralph, Raphael, or anything else he wants. They didn't know Clyde, but that he was a picaroon ghost who made it to heaven is fantastic. But some don't like his dog, *"Dumb ass is too smart for his own good."*

Ralph's immediate objective as a guardian is to propel his only client to achieve. Hiker's job application is accepted; the acceptance letter is mailed from a government agency. It was submitted many months ago.

And hopefully as Ralph he can continue correcting any of his past mistakes he made when he was a spirit. Hopefully the one his own father made that led to the Hunter being shot is resolved. It was the mistake of giving this foolish youth more at one time than his sad mind could process. Luckily, as Morris drives him up the mountain to his family, Hunter is getting a second chance.

Then there is this intellectually enhanced canine living with them whose name is either *"Dog"* or *"Dumb ass."* Ralph has scant obligation to the animal because Ralph's father created this problem. Even though Dog once saved Hiker from being murdered by three thugs. The oddest coincidence is- one of those thugs was Malcolm, Hunter's long lost brother. Fortunately Mal has turned to the Lord for salvation. Hopefully, he will share his mothers' love with Hunter who is about to renew his relationship with Grace and Mal. It's a complicated problem.

Hunter hasn't always been a sterling human being to the dog either... When Hunter was its' master, Dog certainly didn't think he was. So he left Hunter to see the world. Lucien tells Ralph in disgust, *"At this moment Dumb ass is chewing on a duck he stole from a hunter down in the marsh!."*

It's one he pilfered by befriending a duck hunter. Pretending to be this duck hunters' new best friend. Duck retriever Dumb ass hung around until the hunter dropped one. More rapidly than the shooters' own retriever could move, Dog scarfed it up and fled with the morsel.

When it comes to eating anything, this animal will always be his own best friend... Still he is extremely loyal to Hiker and Angela. Although Dumb ass can see Ralph and Lucien, he just tolerates them. He thinks, *"They just don't smell bad enough to be real people!"*

Neither Dog nor Hunter were very bright when they started out. Vigilante's father, Spirit experimented with him using some weird power he had to boost the dogs' intellect to overcome domination by Hunter, then the dogs' master. An unexpected consequence is a part of Spirit's meddling nature also rubbed off on Dumb ass as well.

Dumb ass's daily prowl takes him several miles from the family. On several occasions, on his circular route, he observed two neighbors arguing. Since then, whenever he sees a package on eithers' front porch he carries it to the other's. They agree with one another about how stupid the drivers are who get the addresses wrong when they return parcels to their opposite. Being just a dog, he doesn't know why, it just makes him feel good when they agree with one another even on one thing.

Angel Ralph not only has this dog to contend with at the big house, one who doesn't really understand, he's the third incarnation of the Will Gold spirit. And this was Will Gold's home. Then there's also Lucien's really spooky avian associate, a raven. It's a deceptively powerful one who saved the day at the angels' wedding when the demon Strangler tried to steal the bride.

This same Raven creature by some innate power destroyed the last thread of that evil spirit. Raven kicked the unearthly stuffing out of the evil *Strangler* all of the way down to hades. Before this day is over, Raven will destroy another demon.

The dog finds everything about his adopted family very mysterious. He doesn't care to worry about it although he's very clever for a dog. His immediate concern is his fleas. His hindleg paw bats him behind his ear; being super smart doesn't mean his fleas are any kinder. He worries mostly about the valuable time he wastes scratching and biting back at those little sons of bugs.

Fortunately for all in the household, even though he is smart and can see and hear angels he doesn't sense that Lucien's husband was Vigilante Spirit. The reason: it seems a slip of that ones' mind was overheard with Dog's least favorite nickname- *Dumb ass*.

None of the living can determine how soon the new danger will arrive including Dog. And none of the immortals are allowed to stave it off. *"It's nearby,"* observes Lucien. And while they as guardian angels, can't directly intervene, they are allowed to alert their clients. If they can, Angela and Hiker should be able to defend against whoever or whatever evil comes after them. Lucien has been helping Angela learn how to defend herself.

Even so, an ethical problem haunts her. At the guardian angel level, they may not kill human beings. Their mission is to try to help human beings to exist within a state of grace. That means to follow the commandments.

As unlikely as it may seem, they have no directive concerning clones. Lucien believes they must treat clones the same as they would natural twins until new orders come down. The fact twins are God's creation and clones are partly mans' aberration leaves this question in limbo.

"The problem becomes even thornier with cyborgs." Ralph suggests. But for now there are no demonic cyborgs anywhere close to Angela and Hiker. *"We can't solve every question by just shooting from the hip, complains Gee. Some questions are for the Almighty to reveal to us at His pleasure."*

Raven listens with interest but has her own agenda. She stealthily floats on a soft breeze to a lake on the property. It is where the late Will Gold lost his life. There is no way the demons could have caused an upstream earthen dam to wash him over a waterfalls. But, a demonic crow sensed his danger in a critical moment before Raven. It intentionally distracted her causing her to fail in her duty to sound an alert in time for hapless Will to avoid his demise.

This foul crow sits on the same branch and doesn't sense Raven is about to send him down to hell. A loud "CAW" and a final shrill scream of terror. Raven has exacted justice. Only a few crude black feathers remain to flow down the stream.

4

INHERITANCE

Her trip to the mailbox announces a huge property tax assessment is payable. Angela wells up in with tears when she sees the amount and shows it to Hiker. Summing up their individual checking account balances is depressing. They realize as he sadly states, *"Even \ combining both of our cash* *resources we are considerably short of what we need to pay our property taxes."*

Until this bit of reality came crashing in the two lovers beleived they could live on love alone as young lovers do. Any shortage of money is a rotten surprise. *"How are we expected to pay this much?"* *"They've got to be kidding!"* *"This is outrageous!"*

After their fury subsides survival mode sets in. Hiker anxiously points out the obvious. He wails, *"Everything in our home belongs to you."* *I realize the accident wiped out your memory."* *"And my clearance with the agency hasn't come through yet, so the money in my checking account is all I have for now."* *"Still there must be money somewhere."* *"Do you have any idea where to look?"*

"What clearance?" *With what agency?"* This is the first she's heard her husband is looking for work. He explains he hasn't wanted to mention his application to a nearby government agency because he might be ashamed if he was rejected. He adds, *"You know I have a degree in*

cybersecurity...right?" "It's hanging on our bedroom wall." She lies with a disarming smile, *"Of course, I'm proud of you."*

In reality, the last thing Angela looks for in the bedroom is what's on the wall. "I'll bet you don't know the name of my school." She's in dangerous territory, so she admits she doesn't. He soothes her with, *"Little wonder, the school changed its' name." "It says, UMUC but after almost three quarters of a century it change its' name to UMGC." "Now It is now University of Maryland Global College."* She doesn't care why; the important thing is she's off of the hot seat in this discussion.

His mind moves in a more productive direction. With her guardian angels' help Angel recalls something she never knew. *"Maybe I can remember; follow me."* She leads him to her fathers' old study. It's a dormered room in the attic they haven't discovered. He hopefully follows her up extremely narrow stairs to a landing then through a narrow door.

The ancient amber floorboards squeak in protest. They find themselves standing before the desk where her late fathers' computer has been running constantly before and since his death. It displays only its' screensaver.

Hiker taps the keyboard. Will Gold's machine faithfully demands his password. This magic word is one neither can imagine. Looking down, Angela spies a tiny yellow sticky note barely hidden on the front of the drawer. The scrawled writing reads, *1nGodwetru$t*. At first she doesn't get its' meaning. She smiles as she realizes it's the key and points to the tiny square. Hunter shrugs and starts keying in the letters, number, and symbol, *"Nothing beats a try like a failure."*

Hunter mumbles, *"His password isn't very sophisticated.."* Then in a more apologetic tone. *"But when he created this word I'm sure your father couldn't have imagined he'd be dead, and we'd be standing here trying to break into his stuff.."*

That phrase strikes both funny. Angela tries to remember something nice about her father and comes up with nothing.

The desktop opens with the warning the virus definitions are out of date. They impatiently wait for the updates as their anticipation boils over. He's especially excited over a folder titled *-PWs.*

But this excel sheet is also secured by its' own password. Hunter thinks for a moment then says- *"The birth certificate you found says you were born on September 1st, 2001 right?"* She nods affirmatively. He tries *912001*; the folder opens revealing many other passwords. Another unsecured folder opens. It's loaded with bank icons. They can see everything.

Although when Will Gold was alive, he displayed little to no emotional attachment to this biological daughter, on some weird cold digital level he did. Angela feels a very strange sense of something she doesn't recognize in herself. *"Maybe I was loved?"* Lucien sheds a sad tear for Angela thinking, *"Sorry- wishful thinking!"* *"Your father was only interested in himself."*

As they look over the long list of id's, passwords, and account numbers, they see that all of the accounts involving stocks and bonds were closed just before his death. Hiker points to an open account- *"This bank located just outside of town seems like a convenient place to start."* Angela looks at the account balance in utter shock and quickly realizes she doesn't need to look for a job. They run downstairs and celebrate.

Next afternoon's mail brings good news for Hunter. A registered letter arrives confirming his security clearance has finally been approved. It's for the classified position he applied for months ago at that government agency. Surprisingly, he will be picked up and taken to his place of employment. Promptly at 6:00 am a staff car picks him up at their front door. Neither says a word along the way.

Angela is alone in her big house for the first time since Hiker showed up at her doorstep asking to use her outside spigot to refill his canteen, Angela wanders back up to the office in the attic. Reopening her fathers' ledgers, she realizes just how wealthy she is.

The bank accounts all have the same ID and password. Each opens disclosing balances in the billions. Several overseas are in euros and pounds. Angela hasn't any idea what to do with all of this money. She must learn…

A popup ad offers a trial subscription to the Wallstreet Journal for only one dollar. She accepts the offer. Although she doesn't remember how to drive a car, she quickly figures out how to download ride sharing apps. Angela is going to town! Lucien worries, *"I'm going to have my hands full keeping her out of trouble!"* Ralph laughs, *"It's going to be fun just watching both of you!"*

Later in the afternoon, the same drab pool car returns to the house and Hunter is dropped off.

Nearly hidden in a stack of new clothes, she asks, *"What did they tell you today?"* He is elusive saying, *"It's all on a need to know basis."* She feels rebuffed. Angela decides- *"If he's got secrets then the full extent of our wealth is also going to be on a need to know basis as well."*

The other husband of this house on the hill has

problems as well. Poor Ralph never knows when or whether Raven is watching them. He suspects she's overly curious. After all, as newlyweds, Ralph and Lucien need their privacy. But even now, he isn't quite sure why because as he tells his wife, *"Things with angels happen awfully fast."* And that brings up the subject of what being married to another angel is about.

Even now, Ralph finds it all confusing. Things just don't just happen they way he thought they would before they got married because angels just don't produce offspring in the manner of living people …something similar to the immaculate conception... Ralph says, *"I just can't even think about it."* *"Raven hears my every thought."*

And then there is Dog. An odd thing about dog and raven is their mutual attraction. On the surface, Raven resembles any other bird of her species. Dog sees beyond her façade and understands Raven is much more… an angel! *"But what kind of angel wastes her time being a raven?"*

As Raven's mentor, Lucien never discusses the subject with Ralph much less Dog. She feels it's harder to explain than the differences that stood in the way of her relationship with Ralph when he was Vigilante an echo spirit. When Gee stops by on his way to gather souls she mentions this to him. The Grim Reaper laughs. When he leaves she rolls her eyes, *"Men!" "Why even bother to talk to them?"*

But something else he told her is interesting. The grim reaper visits hell frequently. It seems the devil is outraged that another good angel has been anointed. The devil feels cheated because no new fallen angels are possible. Gee says, *"He's threating revenge."* Lucien shrugs it off because- *"He just can't accept the fact he lost!"*

Raven's instruction and grooming are complete. Lucien feels it's time for Raven to be elevated. She clears it with the next higher level and announces Raven's graduation party. A historic restaurant just downstream in Elkridge is chosen because it has a beautiful welcoming garden where weddings are often held. Historic Elkridge town has ghosts older than Methuselah. But that's a tale of another time.

This celestial graduation merits a ceremony befitting a sacrament. Raven chooses her minister; it's Gee, the same as when Lucien and Vigilante Spirit wed. Gee is beside himself with joy over the honor.

The amount of time it takes to transport souls either way is so insignificant his absence from the ceremony won't be apparent. But, when Gee wants to honor or terrify a soul he summons his ship the *El Muerte* and it seems to take forever. No of that today. Raven is becoming an exalted seraphim angel

This commencement is completed without an objection from angels or invasion by demons. In fact there are very few guests due to Raven's essentially unsocial nature. Surprisingly, a lovely young angel emerges from her feathered identity. Raven isn't a guardian angel; so none are here. She is an exalted proud *seraphim 1st class*. Soon she is ready to leave for her celestial home but hesitates to leave. She has spent so much time perched on chimneys she wants to sit inside to get the feel of what it's like.

Lucien is delighted with her students' accomplishment. But there are no sad farewells; for Raven's transformation is a joyful evolution. These vastly different angels won't see one other and have no common destiny. If in a thousand years they happen to cross paths again, it could be as if they never met. Both just did what was expected, no more or less. Dog sheds the only tears of sadness and sets out for a long walk. He really likes Raven and hates to lose her companionship. *"I'm going to miss her."*

Unfortunately for Dumb ass dog though, this is the very last time Raven will be able to spend time with Lucien. She asks for a quick discussion about Dog. Raven has been under Lucien's control during her orientation to understand humankind. However Raven, was always destined to become a fully-fledged seraphim. Still, she empathizes with the dogs' problem of being so smart he enjoyed hearing the writings of Tolstoy she recited from the chimney.

A seraphim has significantly higher rank in the hierarchy of angels than Lucien and Ralph, especially the latter. This a request Lucien must honor. The seraphim assumed the form of an avian only to gain awareness of the problems humans create for themselves and their world through incivility and worse.

Two classy angels stop everything to discuss one raggedy flea-bitten dog, Raven loves him and is extremely emotional over leaving her *Dumb ass*. Raven refers to his obvious disability, *"Although Dog has no human DNA, he was carelessly infused with way too much intelligence."*

The seraphim pretends concern whether this animal is safe enough for humankind. For example when Angela and Hiker have the baby Angela doesn't realize she will have next year. Raven suggests an experiment to Lucien to test Dumb ass dogs' true nature. Actually Raven wants to confiscate him.

Lucien listens. Regardless of the seraphim's prior status as a two winged earthly creature, all seraphim's have six wings compared to Lucien's two... With six wings, the angel temporarily a Raven, has considerable angelic status. She now deserves respect. Ralph wonders why they need wings at all but doesn't dare to think out loud.

Later when Lucien tries to explain why six wings are important to Ralph, she can only say, *"Angels were around way before airplanes were invented..."* He merely condescends, *"I understand."* But he really doesn't. Angela quips, *"It's like* Hiker when says, *"It's all on a need to know basis."*

Dogs' morning walk carries him to a fork in the road. As with humans, there are always two possible paths for one to travel...a high road and a low road. The low one would take him down to the marshland, where as a lowlife, Dog might steal another duck. The high road leads back to where he as an altruistic Dog manipulated the two feuding neighbors into cooperation and making peace.

The two angels agree to a test. If Dog follows the low road he will be kept outside chained to a doghouse all winter. But if he takes the high road, he will be allowed to live in the house with Angela and Hiker. Lucien assures Raven she can convince Angela to go either way based on the outcome.

Dog trots pensively up to the fork in the road. He lifts his muzzle. He quivers in serious contemplation. His nostrils sample the wind as though trying to sniff out which path to follow. Then with a hearty *"Woof!"* Dog takes the branch leading up the hill. The two angels are happy. Any offer to "take the beast off of your hands by Raven has been undercut.

The former Raven departs forever for the celestial regions. Dumb ass Dog, who heard their entire discussion, grins at his cunning, *"If I repeated my* **steal your duck stunt** *two days in a row, that ticked off shooter might have eaten me for dinner!"* *"Even worse, it gets awfully cold outside in the winter."* *"Hmm, I wonder if any new duck hunters are shooting down in the marsh?"*

Although the two angels are now far apart they each stifle discreet smiles. While Dog is pleased with himself, as Raven departed he sensed something sneaky going on. He sniffs the air again but nothing in the wind seems ominous near the big house. Dog decides to stay closer to home for a while … just in case. In time he will wish he inspected the area near the house much more closely.

Demonic mortals are close by. Dog doesn't know where or when evil is coming but if a threat occurs is ready to protect his family or perish. Little does he suspect the perish aspect is very possible. His happy humans are oblivious to danger.

And while impending drama is about to unfold here, love is about to bloom in the weirdest way. Another couple, Clyde, and Christie was deeply affected by their unworldly past.

5

CHRISTIE & CLYDE

Clyde was a less than sterling ghost who ended up nicely with Ralph's intervention. As a novice pirate, back when he died over a century ago, Clyde was a poor candidate for eternal bliss. Yet Ralph convinced Gee to carry him there.

Clyde is so lonely he has become miserable even in heaven. As a picaroon ghost Clyde encountered Ralph at sunken Oriole Island haunt. It was back when Ralph was still called Vigilante. Clyde barely made heaven. He wouldn't have made it on his own. He got in due to an eleventh hour reprieve from the grim reaper. But he isn't happy here because he doesn't have Christie. So droopy Clyde mopes around heaven pining for his love, his one and only Christie. St. Peter decides Clyde needs to go back and try again.

St. Peter finally negotiates, *"Admittedly Clyde, the spot you've landed in here is not the best place in heaven. But, consider how close you came to the alternative." "And honestly you're dragging heaven down the way you're moping around." "Every other soul up here is happy."* Clyde picks at his tarnished secondhand halo and asks, *"What good is being in heaven without the woman I love?"*

St. Peter warns Clyde, *"We can send you back, but you have to realize you have the risk of messing things up." "You could sin so bad you could go to the other eternity." "Once you are back there, you will lose most of your memory of being here." "Worse for you, her mother who just got here tells me Christie has been seeing someone new..."* Clyde mutters, *"Agreed."*

Undeterred by heavenly celestials heralding his stupidity, Clyde finds himself sitting on a public bench close to where he imagines Christie might pass on her way to the market. He feels her *someone new* will be history once he convinces her to dump the loser. *"He's just trying to find the treasure Clyde knows so well."* A familiar figure walks by; for a moment he thinks it's Christie. But, it isn't. Still, he admires the scenery. With no idea of modern cosmetics he thinks *"I wonder why girls look so much better than they used to?"*

Fortunately, he has been returned to the 21st century with a new wallet and enough money to transition into Christie's world. Even with adequate funds, he's about to encounter a reality which no one could imagine back in his crude era of piracy and debauchery. Clyde had it rough when he was wanabee pirate. Christie's roguish world will seem confusingly smooth.

Sitting here in the Annapolis sun was pleasant the first day. But today his backside has become weary and sore. Patiently he shifts from side to side on his ever harder bench. Clyde squats gingerly from one butt cheek to the other. As the sun goes down and the second day ends, he realizes his bottom hurts really bad. And because he hasn't budged the local police are increasingly focused on him. The cop thinks, *"He's rubbing his ass." "He must be alive."*

But, thanks to heavenly tailoring he doesn't appear to the constabulary to be a vagrant. For some unknown reason he finds a paper with an address in his wallet. He realizes it must be where Christie came home to when she was rescued. It was her mothers' home here. Finally his backside is intolerably painful. He's had enough sitting and waiting. *"Christie, where are you?"* He gets up and something starts guiding him.

Stiffly limping through the residential area, Clyde comes to a red brick building and sees a sign saying *Room for Rent.*

Standing before the door he's uncertain as to what to do next. It opens. Clyde is face-to-face with Christie the girl he came back from heaven to be near. She pauses thoughtfully, *"He seems awfully familiar."* *"But I don't remember his name."* Christie smiles. She asks, *"Are you here about the room my mother was planning to rent?"* *"My mom passed away several weeks ago."*

Christie takes his frozen grin for a yes. She says, motioning with her hand, *"Come in, and decide for yourself whether or not you find it suitable."* *"That room was my business partners', but we broke up, and I no longer need so much space."* He says, *"I'll take it!"* He hands her his new wallet. *"Take whatever it costs."* He doesn't know the value of the paper money much less a reasonable rent. Christie removes several bills from his wallet and hands it back. They don't discuss the term of this lease. It won't matter.

"How soon do you want to move in?" His eyes drop bashfully as he ask *"Now if it's possible? I've just arrived in town. "I don't have a place."* She agrees. *"Do you have your luggage with you?"*

Almost on cue, there's a knock at the door. Christie opens it and is greeted by a uniformed chauffer. A long black limo waits at the curb with its' truck open. *"May I carry in your luggage now Sir?"* Astounded at the timing, but impressed, Christie answers for flabbergasted Clyde, *"Bring the bags up; I'll show you where to put them."* The chauffer obliges and without further conversation leaves. They are alone; the moment is wonderful for both. But only Clyde knows why.

If Christie was astounded by the timing of the luggage, Clyde was even more. Every move he has made since arriving has been spontaneous. Something in the room capture his attention. He stares up at an electric lamp on the dining room wall. It appears to be a torch.

But it's a modern reproduction. It has an eerie resemblance to one he and his friend Vigilante kept burning for Christie when Clyde was the ghost of Oriole Island. It flickers... Christie sees him staring at the electric candle and chills envelop her from her head to her toes. Suddenly she knows. Christie whispers in a shaky voice, *"I had it made to my specifications."* He knows; she knows…they know one another.

Neither dates acknowledge the obvious. The tension is too great. *"Can I buy you dinner?"* She accepts and soon they are waiting to be seated in an old restaurant uncomfortably near to *that* bench. The one whose hard planks are permanently embossed upon his backside.

The policeman whose suspicions were aroused mere hours ago now watches Clyde with awe. He wonders how Clyde got so lucky with a girl as beautiful as this by just sitting on that bench. He decides he'll sit there too on his day off. *"Maybe I should get so lucky?"*

After a short wait, they find themselves seated near a large burning fireplace. Clyde explains he has just come from spending some time in a large religious community and isn't familiar with the kinds of food found on a modern restaurant menu. Although he lived by the sea and on the bay, he can't imagine what's in a Chesapeake platter. So he accepts her offer to order for him.

This will be the undoing of Clyde's mystique because she starts by ordering them both vodka oyster shooters. For all of the wine he as an invisible ghost supplied to Christie for her survival from the sunken treasure cavern, Clyde never took even a sip.

He jubilantly remembers the taste of oysters though. Ignoring the vodka, he washes them down as fast as he can. Soon he feels weird. *"Lord, please don't make me a ghost again right now; I'm having too much fun!"* The other patrons think he's being witty, and all applaud. Christie pays their waiter and leave. Clyde isn't walking well; his knees are numb.

Christie's place is only a few short blocks from the restaurant. However, Clyde is exhausted from being without sleep and oyster shooters. If the same limo didn't pulled up to the curb Christie would need to hail a taxicab because Clyde can barely walk.

Those vodka oyster shooters don't help Clyde's navigation. If the chauffer weren't waiting to help him up the steps Clyde would still be on her front steps. She realizes belatedly her dinner date isn't the sophisticated man he might seem.

"And why can't I remember much about him?" Her sainted mother tries to yell down at her- *"Because Clyde was a dam ghost!"* But Christie doesn't care to listen. By the time he reaches his bed he's fast asleep. She leaves a small nightlight and the bathroom light on. Hopefully, he will be able to get there in time.

Christie remains perplexed about this and other things about Clyde. But, just like when they were back in the cave where she somehow met him, without really seeing him, she simply accepts his bizarre nature.

While she is willing to overlook his strange nature, Christie realizes where he's concerned, *"Abnormal is the new normal."*

Christie awakens at the first light of morning. This is the earliest she's been awake since her mother died several weeks ago. She peers out of the front window to see if the mysterious limo is at the curb, no sign of limo or driver. Tiptoeing quietly, she peeks in at Clyde.

No sign of life here either. Little wonder, this is the first sleep he's had in more than a century. Christie thinks, *"This dude snores like a constipated lion."* Sunrays illuminate his bare red backside shining up at the ceiling. She observes his blisters from sitting so long and the imprint of the bench and giggles quietly, *"Clyde is so patriotic; he has the Stars and Stripes tattooed on his backside."* A bawdy invisible ghost whispers to her, *"Flip him over to see if he stands at attention."*

She quickly slips on her jogging clothes and sets off down the street for an early run. *"I feel really great!"* But as she walks quietly back into the house, she can hear Clyde praying, *"Dear Lord if you make my head feel better, I promise I'll never drink vodka again."*

After her shower, they sit at her kitchen table eating the light breakfast. She pretends she didn't hear his hungover misery. He takes coffee for his first time with four sugars and lots of cream. Clyde's first hangover he hopes will be his last one. But only time will tell.

He realizes she now understands he was in the cave with her. Because her rational mind can't digest the truth. The truth being: back in that cave Clyde was a ghost. To remain sane her mind needs a sane alternative. So, she very nicely ask him, *"Clyde, why didn't you say anything?" "Why didn't you talk to me when we were in the cave?"*

Clyde lies convincingly, *"I had a really bad case of laryngitis; with all of that moisture in there my voice was completely shot." "You incessantly sang Proud Mary Keeps Rollin and shivered so hard that you couldn't hear me whenever I tried to talk to you."*

He doesn't bother to mention the fact invisible Vigilante was there too. This confuses her into a nearly rational state of mind. After awhile she suspiciously tells him, *"I couldn't even see you.*" He accuses her, *"I not only saw you, I held you in my arms." "You just weren't paying attention to me!"* She seems to remember being held.

He gives her a somewhat haughty glance and says, *"After the twelfth oyster shooter last night I didn't see you either."* She's taking this in and Clyde's on a roll. *"Do you understand, from the moment we rescued you, or I should say I rescued you, your only liquid intake was wine?"*

She thinks to herself, *"This is the only thing that makes sense, but why did he start to say WE?"* They decide not to bring up the subject again, especially not today. They enjoy their time together without any idea who the other really is or the others' true being. Annapolis ghosts follow them around. One states. *"If there is going to be a wedding, it's not going to be one made in heaven."* Another agrees, *"Amen!"*

Fantasy may not be an ideal state, yet Clyde feels just to be with her is as heavenly as he wants. She has no idea how she really feels about Clyde. Christie doesn't think she's in love, but she finds him very warm and interesting.

She whispers, *"You're just like a child seeing everything for the first time."* He looks into her eyes and smiles confidently. He is thankful she cannot read his mind as he thinks, *"I have no idea how to behave or what I am supposed to do next!"* *"Where is the town well?"* *"Where is all of the water coming from?"* *"There is no outhouse."* *"Where are the horses and mules?"* *"Why didn't that lamp burn?"* *"Christie is beautiful."*

She does hear him ask- *"I think I'm gonna be sick..."* Christie points to the bathroom and shouts, *"Hurry hurry, the bathroom's that way!"* He peers deeply into the round toilet bowel thinking, *"So that's the well."* And then he dumps his lunch into that well. *"Boy is Christie going to be angry!"* He rinses his mouth without raising his head..

6

EVIL COALITION

Back at the big house in Elkridge its' quiet, Raven has gone to her permanent assignment. From Ralph comes a sigh of relief. As did Roman, Raven felt Lucien married beneath her station. On the human side of the hidden dimension, the side visible to mortals, the couple is happy. A sense of wellbeing hangs over their hill. Nothing signals either couple that clones and crooks are coming after them …but they are ….

Two displaced denizens of Wallow's dirty alleyways meet to plot a burglary. They were told of the big house by a nasty barmaid whose daughter unknown to her became Angela. It wouldn't matter to her even if she knew. She thinks when Will Gold washed over the dam one day the house was sold to some young couple with money. Information she could sell for a share of the take.

Burglars, robbers, and thieves loved the squalor of old Wallow and hate their easy ways of extracting loot. These foul creatures are jealous of anyone's hard earned gain. Rather than honor them by some form of combat, Gee solves their problem by sending them down before they can work out the details of their wickedness. Lucien and Morris work out the details using methods outside the norm.

As Gee drops off these lost souls at hell, Satan's fury is threatening. The devil demands God the father, impeach his only son Jesus or else he will resume the battle he lost. Gee is the fearful bearer of the threat. As always the Grim Reaper tries to straddle the middle ground in some eternal struggle of good and evil. He has to get along with both; neither appreciate his work.

Another threat is no less serious; mortal opponents are arriving as human clones. Three are doubles of: Hiker, the Director, and a woman the angels don't recognize. Two ghosts from their haunt on another hill tell Lucien the cloned identity of only the first two. These friendly apparition can't identify anyone who the female impersonates.

This leaves Lucien to ask, *"If you don't know who then how you know she's a clone?"* They only shrug and repeat their observation. One pouts, *"They just aren't normal."* Rather miffed at being doubted, they take leave of the big house. Then they float down the hill and up the other like great white sheets in the wind. Of course they don't need sheets but feel naked without them.

The angels' attention turns far away toward the mountain. Two evil demons are sneaking stealthily up Grace's. Hatred is the sin of those lacking kindness and generosity. One particular demon has deadly vengeance in mind. His is the decadent spirit of the murderer Buck. It's his evil echo splinter. It erupted when Buck was dying.

In life Buck was the ringleader who instigated an attack on Hiker. While he was running from the wrath of Dog he murdered one of his cronies. One who also beat and tried to rob Hiker. Another of Buck's cronies would have been Buck's next victim had Mal not escaped. Mal's mother found him nearly dead. Her loving care and prayers saved him. Mal recovered and repented. Buck is coming to destroy everyone.

The demons intensely hate the big dog who lives with the two couples. Because not long ago it rebuffed an attack on Hiker. He became vicious because he was possessed by a combination of spirits who nearly caused him to kill the trio of thugs.

Those spirits were the angel Roman and Vigilante's father the echo Spirit. In that episode, the dog went from runaway to vicious and back to loveable. Reflecting, dog wonders why the shock of those transitions didn't destroy him. Unlike other dogs, he analyses his actions..

To no ones' regret except his own evil spirit, Buck died after being run over by an old lady in a Chevy. It was Grace; she couldn't stop her car. After being driven off from their attempt to rob, this criminal she ran over had tried to kill his two partners including her son. Only her son survived to repent. She is still nursing Mal back to normal health. Sensing his life draining away allowed him to understand reality. The loyalty he gave to his friend Buck was wasted on a fiend.

The demons are moving stealthily up the mountain aiming to strike Grace and her sons. Thug Buck was struck so hard by Grace's old car he flew through the air a lot like a kite without a tail. He literally lost his tail as he died a slow and painful death at the bottom of the road embankment. It was an impact hard and sudden.

His was a death was so ghastly an evil echo spirit burst forth from his brain. It was similar in form to the one Angela's father, emitted when he was about to die. Fortunately, her fathers' echo chose to do good.

Buck's lust for revenge is demonic. Roman ruminates *"If old Strangler and Buck got together as a pair they might beat us!"* Angela poofs, *"Bullfeathers!"* *"I'd love to battle both at one time."* Ralph chuckles to himself, *"So this is the quiet deliberative guardian angel I married?"* *"Double bullfeathers!"*

The only difference between the two demons is the echo spirit of Strangler tried to destroy Angela and Lucien. As demonic and just as cruel, Buck's spirit hates Grace and Mal. Roman tells Gee, *"Buck's is just as evil as was his mortal mind when it emitted his demon."*

Gee orders, *"Go get them Roman; I'll be standing by to carry them home..."* Then realizing he's plagiarizing a line from an old hymn, he adds- *"... and I won't be swinging low with a sweet chariot either." "I'll be slinging hot lead from The El Muerte."*

By himself Buck would eventually just fade away. However, another a new subordinate has joined forces with him. This one is also a hater seeking revenge indiscriminately against everyone and everything. He's Buck's newest sycophant and lets Buck think for him. Which considering Buck's history with such toadies, isn't very smart.

This sad creature is one whose existence came about during a reversal of fortunes for the promoters and fans of a dog fighting contest. As with most, the loser dog is killed. This spirit managed to erupt in a similar was as echoes are born. They either burst forth at the moment of death or by merging with another. Both despise all who vanquished them. They stop to strategize halfway up the mountain. Buck argues to continue after Mal, and his family. The demon of the dogfight wants to go after Lucien. They reduce their ferocity by arguing.

Equally hated is the demonic pitbull that tore the dogfight demon apart. But they don't know where to find that one. For now, he'll settle for the death of Ralph's dog. *"After we knock off Grace and her mongrels,"* he tells his cohort, *"We'll go find that son of a bitch they call Dumb ass…"* His partner hisses in agreement. Lucien finds this conglomeration of evil almost confusing, but one they will overcome.

If these aren't bad enough in moments there are more…a third and fourth. These losers are the spirits of two thugs Vigilante Spirit cursed. He encountered them in Wallow's Lizard Alley before he became an angel. After watching them mug a man, he implanted a compulsion to beat one another constantly.

After trying to stay apart when alive they died. The curse followed them. They finally caught up with one another as ghosts and punched their way here. There are no secrets in the hidden dimension; they believe they can get to the one who decreed their curse and make him take it away. As one puts it- *"We just want it to go away!"* Buck says, *"Help us; we'll help you."*

Tw of the four are ghosts; two are mere spirits. Two souls were carried to hades by Gee. The ghosts are in limbo. Alone, none would stand a chance against the protection of guardian angels Lucien and Ralph. Yet together this evil lot agrees to destroy every resident in both the house on Grace's mountain and the home on the hill of Angela and Hiker. The fierce Raven's absence is seen by Buck as weakening the defense... an opening for revenge.

Because they are so near to where Buck met his demise he convinces the others to star t by attacking Mal's mother. After all, although stupid Grace thought he was a deer instead of a thug. In Buck's jaded mind, *"She is to be destroyed!"*

His three cohorts are not the best candidates for the task ahead. Each is deathly afraid of something. Even the two ghosts, who can't stop punching lack any hate for Grace. They are helping Buck to find and force Ralph to take away this curse. But they don't really trust Buck at all.

Buck and the dogfight reversal demon are actually afraid of dogs. The two cursed fighters are afraid of each other.

The fact Dumb ass is far away up at the house in Elkridge, makes it easier to sway them to tackle everyone here on Grace's mountain. Roman sees them all as phonies.

Buck thinks, *"Who's going to stop us- Grace?"* After all Grace is just a helpless old woman. And where does Mal get off with his suddenly having religion bit, especially after helping to beat the devil out of Hunter? His repentance and asking the Lord for forgiveness just isn't right in his eyes. Buck sneers, *"It's bullfeathers to them, not me."*

"We're gonna destroy them!" And so, all four try to figure out how to sneak the rest of the way up the mountain to knock off Grace and Mal. But, suddenly there is a coincidence Buck doesn't expect ...

The limo carrying Hunter home up to the mountain cabin reaches the spot in the road where Grace accidently killed Buck. The brightly lit marks on the road Morris the driver has followed are blocked out by an even larger solid scarlet line. Morris stops the car. Hunter consumes the last of his berries then dozes without trepidation. The driver quietly steps out to follow the line.

Looking down and beyond Morris detects and reports the demonic four. His report is heard by an angel. By sheer coincidence it happens to be Roman, the very angel studying Grace and Malcolm. Roman clearly understands what needs to be done. As the limo nears the cabin Morris awakens his passenger.

The car arrives. Grace and Mal see Hunter step out. For only the briefest moment is there apprehension. Then Grace, Hunter, and Mal run to embrace. There excitement so high they fail to notice the limo depart. Once again, Morris has come through. Roman hasn't let his opportunity pass. He changes the opposition with a suggestion only two can hear.

As they shake hands their curse expires. The two original thugs from Lizard Alley have their curse removed and stop fighting forever. They immediately dissolve into the deep mist drifting slowly down from the mountain. Self-satisfied, Roman continues towards Buck rhyming, *"Two in the mist;*

two left to dismiss.". Buck is in dread. Once more this demon strength is down to only two. Duty done, Morris and limo flow down the mountain and are gone.

7

CHALLENGE

The Lord has summons Gee once again for a special project. He hates mankind's self-destruction. Death should occur naturally. Murdering one another isn't a part of His

Divine Plan for the children of earth. Gee will try; should he fail, he too is doomed.

Decade to decade routine of just serving as the grim reaper and carrying out the routine transfers that come with the job is hectic enough. When Lucien asks whether Gee can survive this challenge, Gee only says, *"The answer rests with friends like you and Ralph."* Lucien promises for both. Ralph mumbles - *"We've been down this road before."*

The Lord instructs Gee to make peace in Wallow, the cesspit of humanity. Gee says, *"Lord, this is harder than the time I was told to wipe pirate scum from the Chesapeake."* The Lord says nothing more to him. Gee departs paradise to follow this quest.

He immediately remembers Clyde and Vigilante his choice mystical duo. Then to his chagrin he realizes neither is capable or completely available. *"It's time to recruit... but where?"* *"How?"*

The residents of Wallow City truly despise how the murder rate keeps climbing and thuggery flourishes. But they don't have the ability to change conditions. Gee's usual duties as a transporter of beings to their final destination are considerably escalated by murders. He isn't a public relations technician; he's more like an enforcer. But life and death are not unfolding as they should in dirty old Wallow.

Vigilante and Clyde, two creatures once helped Gee carry out the Lord's work. Vigilante was an echo spirit then. Clyde was the ghost of Oriole Island. Neither are even in the same form, or as needy as they were back when they kicked out the old Chesapeake Bay pirate ghosts. Clyde was stranded and Ralph as was a fading sprit. Both were desperate. Today they have found love and are happy. Gee has a eureka moment. *"Love is the answer to solving this problem!"*

Gee approaches Ralph and Lucien as friends. After all he was the minister who joined them in matrimony. They also can simplify communication between the hidden and human dimensions. He shares his Wallow problem. Lucien admits, *"I know all about the Wallow problem but haven't a clue where to begin."* *"Ralph understands it better because he has seen Wallow's worst."*

It was Lizard alley where prior to becoming an angel he put a curse on two thugs. These are the same two thugs who just eliminated one another from the Grace's mountain coalition. *"I don't think Wallow's solution is going to be as simple as a curse because their self-annihilation is the worst imaginable curse."* Lucien and Gee nod in agreement. Gee says, *"Keep going Ralph; you may be on to something."*

"Well think about it." *"The more who die, the more their murders kill"* *"Why do they murder?"* *"Because that's what they think they're supposed to do."* *"Two reasons are- they see killing as the answer to every problem on TV, movies and the internet."* *"And, they are taught that they are not supposed to be teased or bullied."*

"Moderate hazing was once the way to bring people with differences to a humble realization they are treading on someone else's thinking." *"Usually the one being teased, or called names, or was intruding on another's territory or was*

being initiated into a group having similar ideals such as a fraternity or even the military." "The initiate usually backed off enough to defuse the irritation." "Or they quit." "Neither party felt it necessary to kill the other." "Admittedly, mistakes were made."

Lucien adds, *"Ralph, I'm sure you will agree there are limits to what a victim should take, right?"* He answers. *"Of course, if the parties can be counseled, fine."* *"Where they are too hotheaded the police should be called."* *"And those who threaten violence repeatedly, should be removed to a secure area for as long as their sick murderous attitude persists."* *"Any law allowing even those who even threaten murder to be released without treatment must be revised!"* *"There are mitigating circumstances that must always be adjudicated though."* *"This is why judges exist."* *"Human beings aren't perfect... obviously neither are angels."*

The three hover in the living room deep in thought. Then the Dog plods in and flops down in front of Gee's chair.

He knows this isn't his problem. Because mankind's problems are the sum of their poor decisions.

Human problems accumulate during times when things are actually less violent. The are allowed to fester by those who believe that just one more element of violence or social change without safeguards is OK and won't hurt anyone. But as even Dumb ass dog realizes, *"Wallow has slipped too far into chaos."*

"Lucien, what's your opinion?" Lucien is normally reluctant to offer up an opinion on so serious an issue. But Gee focuses directly. She can't squirm out of answering and reverts to the obvious. *"My suggestion is non-violence as dictated by the rules given to Moses."*

"It comes down to humans; if they want their children to survive to grow old on this planet they themselves must learn and teach and practice Moses's Commandments." This seems too simple of an answer for Gee. *"How do you make this happen?"* She says, *"It's so easy no one thinks it works."* *"Take for example the mourners of murder victims."*

After a murder, mourners get together, light candles and pray." "The Lord hears and treats these as prayers for the departed, not the living." "It doesn't stop the same thing from happening again the next day to another poor soul." "People send their children to school to prepare them for life. Actually they need to ask for the Lord's help in school just to survive."

"The forces of evil are killing them even in school." "The idea of trying to protect people in schools, at work and play with a few armed guards amounts to too little for the size of the task." "Everyone needs to practice the Commandments and pray to the Lord for answers before the demons destroy, as well as after." Lucien adds, *"If those who feel the need to hurt others could feel the grace of the Lord through a brief prayer each morning think of how many lives could be saved?"*

Gee says, "This is something the Lord needs to help mankind with; it's not something as simple as clearing away demons because evil abounds."

Realizing the significance of something so basic. *"Mankind needs to respect the words of the Lord to strike down mankind's own demons."* Gee says, *"Their failure to obey rules as old as when Moses walked the earth should frighten each of them to their core."* With these sober thoughts they each retreat to a moment of prayer, meditation, and awe.

Before Gee leaves the immortals pause to observe Angela and Hiker. She made homemade shepherd pies for dinner; he brought home cherry ice cream. He smiles and leaves. These mortals are in harmony. If only Wallow families can be as well.

Alone again, the two angels feel some envy because they don't eat. So, Lucien and Ralph talk about their day. Ralph points out- *"Did you notice Gee didn't offer any of his own solutions?"* She explains, *"Gee was surveying... he'll report our opinions."* He asks, *"What then?"* Patiently she explains, *"You and I are just one point of a global statistic."* *"They will put all of his surveys together."* *"Then they decide whether each culture is worthy."*

He's puzzled, *"Worthy enough for what?"* Matter of factify she replies, *"To survive..."* Only now does he fully understand she means the total annihilation of Wallow and all who live there..

Smiling ruefully Lucien points out, *"The last time it was the great flood." "At least we offered solutions; hopefully, the others surveyed do also or it may be nearly time for the Lord to pull the plug again..."* Ralph sarcastically chuckles, *"Or, to spill it over again."*

As usual the Lord isn't letting Gee off easy. Gee is using the same tactic that worked when the Lord demanded he cleared the Chesapeake of pirate ghosts...Gee passes the buck. As Gee was talking to Lucien and Ralph souls who needed to be conveyed were backing up. He usually works while he talks. This is important. Gee covers by making a few more ghosts. He'll close out his ghostly inventory when he isn't as busy. Then there are less critical issues such as what to do with the clones. Clones are keeling all over the place. And they have such undeveloped souls. Fully grown adults have the social development of infant human beings. Gee regrets his inability to grab those responsibly for this abomination and take them to where they belong. He promises himself, *"Their day to meet the reaper will come."*

8

DESTINATIONS

As Lucien and Ralph are working out new and profoundly serious Wallow project, an old one has run its' course. A while back a strong willed teacher and an equally stubborn preacher were interred in the old cemetery. They tortured their neighbor ghosts by constantly arguing. That annoyance was resolved by sending the two to an urban purgatory. One where their highly intelligent minds have been forced to settle their differences. The solution isn't a simple handshake. Both must think and speak with a unified voice. Failure means hell.

Although once quarrelsome, lately they have worked together amicably. Finally their differences, while still real, are discussed in a friendly manner. At last they speak in tones exhibiting mutual respect for the opposite position. Appreciating their progress, Gee feels their trial should be over. Regardless of differences. they speak with only one voice to all who seek them for their wisdom. Sadly, the number of wisdom seekers has all but vanished. Recently, those they encounter feel everything necessary is available on their smartphones. Gee admits- *"Being a sage isn't what it was in the good old days."*

Gee explains to them, *"You each have a choice." "You can go up to heaven now to a mansion at the level you have earned thus far...or, you can work on a vital project here hoping to improve your position up there." "The choice is solely yours and both of you are not required to make the same one."*

The former preacher smiles saying, *"I've trusted in God all of my life and I'm ready to take whatever He has in store for me!"* Gee nods and the minister is immediately elevated.

The teacher thinks and thinks. He decides, *"I'll stick around for now to see if I can overcome my doubts."* "Gee says, *"OK, but you need to know you have already earned a place based upon your virtues in life and willingness to work with the preacher here on the streets of Baltimore in your present state." "You have it made either way."* The teacher persists, *"I'll hang around for awhile and try to be of help." "It can't be worse than teaching high school algebra!"*

Gee explains the teachers' first task is to persuade people to love one another and to turn the other cheek when tormented. The teachers' face drops saying, *"That makes teaching high school seem easy."* Gee quips, *"We won't hold the results against you...Jesus tried it and you see what they did to Him."*

Moments later, the teacher's ghost finds himself hovering over the intersection at the top of Lizard Alley in the loveless city of Wallow. He chuckles and says to anyone listening, *"I'm looking for an easier place to begin." "This reminds me of monitoring school detention."*

He hops onto a dirty green uptown bus towards a healthier neighborhood thinking, *"I'll start at the top and work my way down." "Gee didn't say I had to start at the ground floor." "It's easier to pull people up from the top than from the bottom." "Because everybody down there keeps trying to pull one another down with them."* Gee is amazed, *"I wish I'd thought of that!"* Then he realizes, *"If preacher hadn't opted for heaven, teacher would have."*

On the way back from conveying another soul. Gee decides on his own urban renewal plan. Then Gee frightens the few mortals in Lizard so dreadfully they flee the Alley forever.

As soon as the last mortal is gone, every structure on both sides of the wicked alleyway is torched. Then he guides every evil ghost to misery. Surprisingly, he released several innocent victims who were trapped and now are free.

It is important to mention that no living human beings were destroyed during this obliteration. For as always Gee is a transporter of souls and cannot kill mortals. In Lizard Alley however most of the innocents he liberates are is such wretched condition they soon perish. Two made it to heaven. The land under Lizard Alley is due for serious improvement.

The old *Lizard A*, as locals call it, soon will disappear from memory. When the burning rubble cools it will be demolished and trucked away. As the ashes are cold any who take souvenirs will be cursed. In what way the curse will attach remains to be seen.

9

TOO YOUNG

For all of the excitement in their relationship Christie and Clyde aren't quite right for one another. It isn't for any lack of affection. When he left heaven to come back to her he was revived to the same physical age his body was when he died over a century ago. He is just 17; she's almost 22. His new drivers license shows he's also 22. But compared to her, his emotional immaturity and lack of experience has their relationship becoming unbearable to both.

Clyde has never seen so many young women his own age. As they walk along Main Street in downtown Annapolis he can't keep his head on straight. And, He thinks the way the girls dress today is fantastic.

She watches his reactions and doesn't know whether to laugh or cry. His cheating mind and wandering eyes are so honest. She feels she is more like an older sister than a girlfriend. *"This is nowhere!"*

They have lunch but no more oyster shooters. Christy still has a strong passion for sunken treasure. Even without the wine she realizes she must avoid. Neither know he's living with an unlimited credit card limit at zero interest and no monthly minimum payment. But, seeing the quality of his clothes and the crazy elusive limo that simply shows up, she wrongly believes he's cashing in some of the pirate goods. The same ones she and her diving partner weren't able to find.

He obviously hasn't. When she mentions the treasure over lunch he's happy to tell her finding the underwater cave would be fairly easy. Christie almost falls off of her chair in amazement. Clyde has just become much more interesting to her again. *"Clyde, when can we start?"* He frowns, *"Why would we ever want to go back to that horrible place?"* She just sighs.

\   *"Well Clyde..."* She can't believe he thinks she is too stupid to realize where he's getting his money... *"I saw some nice things down there just going to waste."* He thinks to himself; sweet Christie has a greedy side. She asks, *"Do you know how to SCUBA?"*

Clyde was never in the company of a woman as manipulative as Christie. Her diving buddy, also her shrink, arrives at the boat. Clyde and Dr. Ted meet for the first time.

Only now does Clyde realize they tried without success to find sunken Oriole and its' treasures.

He was told by someone he can't remember there is someone else in her life. Now they're face-to-face. Perhaps because he has such mixed feelings and doesn't have a better plan. He gets their sailboat underway; Clyde is an experienced sailor. That's the only way he got around when he was alive the last time.

It's a bright sunny day on the Chesapeake Bay. Dozens of similar sailboats are chasing one another around in the area just north of the Bay Bridge. Clyde is enjoying the ease of this modern boat compared to those of his time. He tacks and they are heading south with the sun nearly overhead. No other boats seem to follow. Christie is pleased and brings Clyde a soda and Dr. Ted a beer. After a few whispers, the lady and dive buddy, have nothing more to say. After their brief fling they stopped being lovers. Now the only thing their relationship is based upon is finding the sunken treasure. Dr. Ted thinks she's as shallow as Christie finds Clyde. But Christie sees him as a good friend.

The sailboat leans into the wind. The feel of the wind in his face once again is something Clyde has missed. Christie and her partner lick salty spray from their lips in anticipation of finally finding treasure. Dr. Ted tries to record the coordinates. He can't for some reason. It keeps fluctuating. *"What an odd time for this thing to act up."*

Clyde frowns and the sailboat turns slightly to port again and again. At last he drops anchor at a certain spot announcing, *"We are above Oriole Island."* Dr. Ted, her diving buddy helps Christie on with her tank. They cautiously omit putting out the SCUBA flag and are quickly over the side. They descend almost immediately reaching the shallow bottom because the tide is out. Not long ago Oriole Island was a flourishing dry island well above water. And it was fairly large, covering many acres. Christy heads for the side of the house hopefully in the direction of the treasure room.

There is no ghost or other spirit to deter her. The only being who has ever take a proprietary interest in Oriole since it sank is taking a nap in the boat about 20 feet overhead. Clyde is smiling as he dozes only half awake. The entrance to the cave is nearly impossible to find even in full sunlight. Now it's nearly impossible unless you know exactly where to look. Clyde smirks, *"Old man Farthing didn't want people to find it." "Good luck."*

Christie spots something shiny near where she came out when she left before. Scooping it up out of sight of her diving buddy she realizes it was a rather large mine cut diamond she dropped on her way out when she left the first time. She slips it into a pocket on the side of her buoyancy compensator device. *"What was mine is stills mine."* That her idea flies in the face of the fact she is salvaging the property of others doesn't faze her. She just isn't going to share this with the other two.

They brought four bottles of air, which should have given them plenty of time underwater, except when they first arrived on the bottom they were so excited they quickly sucked their first two bottles dry. Both surface to get a second bottle. Clyde asks rather sleepily, *"How's it going?"* Unconsciously touching her BCD pocket, Christie lies, *"Nothing so far."* Clyde just yawns. Dr. Ted sheds his bottle, replaces his and Christie's. Almost instantly they are back over the side.

Not wishing to repeat their air deficiency, and especially important not to be the first to run out while under, they move and breath more slowly. Christie spots a terrapin scrambling into a remarkably familiar opening. This time her partner is able to log the exact coordinates.

They excitedly share this information with Clyde. He just shrugs. He not only knows this location; he knows every piece within the cavern to its' finest dimension. He can see the bulge of Christie's BCD hiding her prize. He just smiles at her. Christie's face turns blood red with the shame of being caught.

10

ROMAN'S CHOICE

Hiker and Angela haven't the slightest idea they live in the same house with their guardian angels. The existence of celestial creatures is so far beyond reason for any human. To know for certain would be insanity. But this is the way the celestial universe is meant to be.

As for Ralph and Lucien, perhaps their focus should be on the two people they reside with. Instead it is far to the west at Grace's mountain. Roman is peeking into the cabin window. There is Grace with her sons. She is reading her bible to them.. Nothing could please him more. He wonders why she needs a guardian angel. But Lucien said so and so he must.

His feels her deep desire to be in harmony with God's will. This sight of the Grace with her sons softens his dislike of Malcolm. Roman has forgiven Mal for hurting Hiker when he was the boys' guardian angel. Still, there is no doubt about his newfound sincerity. Perhaps Grace has enough virtue for all three.

Because he once inspired Dog to maim Malcolm his suspicion remains with him. Yet, lacking the wicked influence of his deceased buddies Mal appears once again to be the good man Grace raised. Ralph and Lucien look on with approval.

Grace's motherly influence is wonderful. For she has provided Mal with the best lesson possible through good example. But deciding who he will serve as guardian must wait. A demonic spirit is near once more. The three angels are so focused on the good, Roman realizes Buck has slipped into the perimeter of safety protecting Grace.

Roman alerts Lucien - *"Before I decide who, if anyone, receives my services as a guardian angel, I need to deal with an immediate problem. "Some evil spirits are here." "One is our old friend Buck." "There's also a really weird one who escaped after escaping from a bloody dogfighting ring." "It hates everything- people, dogs, you name it." "His idea of a good time was watching dogs tear each other to pieces."*

Roman cannot imagine how an echo spirit whose human body was ripped apart by a pitbull can even be a threat to anyone. *"That stupid fool actually bet on the dog who bit him."* Gee happens by and asks, *"Why expect a spirit to be brighter than the person it came from?" "Vigilante Spirit as an echo spirit was exceptional."*

This part of the Vigilante Spirit legacy must still be resolved. It is truly a penance for Roman to even think of the angel Vigilante has become for two reasons. He didn't like Ralph when he was Vigilante Spirit and he remains heartbroken over Lucien's rejection of his advances.

He really hated Vigilante's marriage to Lucien. At that moment Vigilante was elevated to the status of a guardian angel. Still in spite of his bruised feelings, Roman trudges on with his duties as a guardian. He doesn't want to be regarded as a fallen angel besides being a recovering substance abuser.

Outside of his present determination to protect he accepts humility as a penance imposed by Gee and supervised by Lucien. He was self-serving when Roman unmasked Lucien at her wedding. While he may have been truthful, to unmask Lucien posing as Mercy was contrary to his role as a guardian angel. The divine plan has ethics far beyond those of humble Roman. Gee warns, *"Let this be a lesson to all of our dimension." "We don't play by the rules of humankind." "We serve God and mankind."*

Back in the earthly realm, Hiker and Angela will soon realize something about his new position. Neither do enemies of the Agency and the country it serves.

At this moment, the Directors' secretary is leaving the building and the boss she has worked for since graduating from school. She signs out; it will be her last time.

Moments later as she turns her car off the main road on the way to her home a highway worker wearing yellow bearing a hold up a sign reading STOP; so she stops. A face from nowhere appears at the driver side window. She is startled to realize the woman could be her twin. It isn't it's her clone.

The passenger window explodes blowing glass across the seat. An arm pokes in and the door opens. The directors secretary feels her body being dragged out of her car into the back of a SUV with very dark windows. she loses consciousness; this is the last thing she will ever see in this world.

11

TWINS & DEMONS

At around 10 am, Angela gets out of bed and walks into

the kitchen. As usual she sips coffee and watches the birds and squirrels playing outside as she gradually wakes up. One bird in particular interests her today, the big new raven sitting on the shed. It isn't bothered by the way she's stares and doesn't fly over to retrieve the piece of toast she tosses. She thinks it's odd and wonders if it's sick.

Another far different resident also takes notice of the raven. Because it's her latest understudy. For she is Lucien the enlightener. That her name is similar to Lucifer means nothing. She had the name first. Although her husband know, she is in fact older than sin.

Moreover, he name Lucien reflects her vocation. She is a teacher of angels. One student is her husband though he has never come to fully realize anything more about Lucien than his love for her. Lucien directs the new raven to come to her away from Angela's view. However, it will remain nearby until Lucien is finished with him and feels he's ready to move on, as did Raven the seraphim. His true nature is too be shielded from human eyes.

Only Dog is aware he has joined the household. But this new raven can't be called by the name Raven. He will be just called *Bird* for now. A more suitable nickname will make itself known in time.

Lucien finally lets her husband know why she has the name Lucien. Ralph barely nods. His attention is presently split between watching Hiker working at the agency and observing Roman's problem with the demons of Grace's mountain. Lucien isn't surprised the meaning of her name doesn't daunt him. She chalks it up to the fact he is a man and therefor naturally insensitive. She thinks, *"Maybe we'll call you Dumb ass instead of that flea trap out front."*

Dog snores contentedly on the front porch and doesn't require attention from anyone in either the hidden or the human dimensions. So Angela has time to thoroughly assess her domicile. In so doing, she becomes unhappy with the condition of the old place. Lucien decides, *"I'll shape things up!"*

Back when Ralph was just an echo spirit he managed to reunite grown twins together who were unaware of one other.

Now they operate a marginally profitable contracting business always desperate for business. Angela picks up her new IPOD and searches for just such a contractor to restore parts of her home. Amazingly, only one comes up… the twins.

Two very battered pickups arrive. Within a couple of days, painting and carpentry are going at a high rate. When Hiker comes home each night he asks how the work is progressing. She pouts. *"It's great when these two show up"* *"Whenever their wives get lonely they stay home."*

The twins tear out and replace rotten wood, then repaint, Bird discovers he cannot stand the smell of paint. So, Lucien dispatches the new raven on what she feels should be a simple mission. He is sent to help Roman.

Roman greets the young creature with the same charm he exhibited with Ralph. *"I need another pair of eyes like I need a hole in the head."* Bird respectfully declines saying, *"I am required to follow the orders of just one."* Roman gives him what some call *Busy work.* *"OK Bird, I want to fly in a circle around the cabin in a 10 mile radius to see whether there is anything worth reporting."*

Gee has already informed Roman about the remaining two malevolent spirits but doesn't tell Bird. It doesn't take long for Bird to report back, *"Two evil demons are almost here!"*

Meanwhile, back at the big house. The twin contractors have shown up and are working hard. For all of their past faults, working together they are really good craftsmen. So good in fact they have discovered a mysterious anomaly in an outer wall, a portion of the house that bulges was beyond the room inside. Rather than tear open the wall, they immediately inform Angela.

Of course Lucien and Ralph were aware of this hidden room. It's where one of Angela's ancestor used to hide untaxed imports smuggled in sailing ships once able to navigate this part of the river. The honest part was their captains would then transfer pig iron back to foreign ports to maintain ballast.

She had the workers open the room from the inside. There was even false entrance within the old knitting room.

Obviously in olden times the fine ladies of this house were in on the smuggling schemes as well.

The house ghost admits they were especially into beating the tax on everything they could. *"They thought it exciting."*

Suddenly Ralph has become busy because Roman and Bird are wondering around Grace's mountain with demons on the loose there. The Twins are working on the hidden room. And he is worried Hiker is in a risky business.

Now a notorious ghost considers the room to be a part of his territory. Ralph tells Lucien not to worry; I've been through this once before. *"Ghosts are all just Boo!"* Plus, Hiker is going through the most hazardous part of his classified training. Ralph moans, *"Just sitting anticipating trouble is worse than fighting pirates!"* Lucien has her own worries.

The ghost problem is the contractor twins have invaded the haunt of a ghost killed here back in 1864 during the war between the States. His family and friends were with the North; he fought on the Confederate side. This was his fiancés' home. He surreptitiously came to visit her late one night while her wounded Yankee brother recuperated in the very room where the fiancé normally slept.

When the wounded yankee saw a Confederate soldier hugging and kissing him in the dark he slipped a knife from the mattress and slit the intruders' throat. The tragedy of it was before the War they were friends.

When morning came the family was in shock. It seemed only prudent to stash this dead Rebel in this convenient hideaway until he could be buried in the garden. The unfortunate soldiers' body wasn't buried because the family suddenly had to flee for their lives.

The dead lover had confided his destination to a fellow soldier. By the time, the war was over his intended was wed to a friendly yankee she met in Philadelphia where the family settled. The sad one who killed him died from his infected wounds. Never did he disclose his one-time friends' fate. The house was sold to Angela's great-great grandfather; it passed down generations and none were wiser.

The mistaken lovers' corpse was never removed from the sealed off room. Nor was he transferred to his ultimate destination due to Gee's oversite. With 50 thousand dead from the Antietam- Sharpsburg alone there were too many at one time for the grim reaper to track.

Lucien pacifies the ghost by asking Gee for a good eternity. Gee apologizes to the ghost but warns, *"I don't make these decisions; Saint Peter controls the pearly gates."* Then Gee and the soldier are gone.

So, Bird, is on his own as two demonic spirits confront Roman, Grace and her sons on the mountain. There is a bit of a problem. They aren't authorized.

A technicality of the mountain situation is that Grace and her sons are not guardian angel serviced at this moment. While that could change if Roman would approve of any or all of them. Lucien warns Ralph, *"This guy is a stickler for protocol."*

Lucien moans, *"To Roman, Not Serviced means they could all drop dead and he might not lift a wing to help."* Bird is on the scene; he could rip both demons apart. But Bird must follow Lucien's direction. But Lucien doesn't react. Bird takes it on himself to bluff the demons.

Planting himself directly between the two and Grace's cabin, he puffs up his chest and stares them down with his fiercest glare. The demons move forward. Buck's spirit hates Grace especially for running him over on the road, Mal, for not dying after Buck tried his worst and Hunter, just for good measure. His maniac associate, the spirit of the pitbull fiasco just wants to hurt everyone.

Bird can't come into contact with them without authorization but mentally confuses both with deep throated raven blare at such a level neither can hear the other. Within the roar of raven rumble he blasts, *"You both are going to hades even if you back off."* They shiver in terror.

"There are two open spaces down there, one for each of you." *'The first one I destroy gets the penthouse where it's just a slight bit cooler."* *"The second will drop immediately into the pit."* *"The pit is deeper, hotter than hell and where hell's*

septic goes." "Those poor devils are always up to their chins; the word of the day every day in the pit is- "Don't make waves!" Bird then appears to lurch at them. Both demons scatter down opposite sides of the mountain. Ralph thinks Bird must have played football; Lucien does cartwheels back at the house; Roman smiles for the first time since he quit sniffing bubbles.

Roman orders Bird back home giving him high marks. As he lands on the porch at the house, even Dog greets him with respect. Lucien smiles but reminds him this is just the beginning of his training. She says, *"What would you have done it they saw through your bluff and attacked you?"* Bird looks away and says, "No *one said I can't defend myself."* She gives him a withering look, then decides to upgrade his name and shorten his course. For the rest of his stay he will be respectfully called- *Hawk.* On the other hand, poor Dumb ass dog doesn't expect much respect in either dimension.

Angela's home restoration is finished. The contractors and their pickups have gone. A newly discovered room is assigned as the refuge for both the retriever and the raven. Although the bird is still youthful, the dog is becoming elderly. Dog finally has a place out of the weather; Hawk shares space with him as an honored guest. Its' lonely ghost is glad to finally have guests. Each has tales to share.

Far to their west and hidden away trouble brews. Lurking within deepest haze, Buck's evil spawn has enemies to hate. But his would be coalition cohort, the one who fled the pitbulls has given up completely. Most of this fools' strength was lost in fright. Up on the mountaintop Roman growls and snarls at Buck, *"Run with all you have Buck...your pathetic coalition is no more; it's just you now."* "You are all alone!"

After watching Grace, her sons and all of the good she has accomplished. Roman has made his decision concerning who gets guardian angel services. He will announce it at dawn. All is silent on the mountain and not a cloud sheds a teardrop.

Chapter 12

CLYDE'S CONFUSION

Within the human dimension, life goes on. Christie and Dr. Ted, her partner, are obsessed with finding Oriole Island's sunken treasure. Clyde has no interest in what he sees as the *pile of trash* he was forced to coexist with for so long. For him, pirate treasure is much less interesting than even an oyster shooter. Besides, the magic card in his new wallet buys everything. He pushes in into a box and they give him whatever he wants. He does remember to say- *"Thank you."*

Dr. Ted and Christie don't need him now. They know their way back to the island. So when Christie wants to go back early Sunday morning he wishes them luck. They head to where their boat is docked.

As everywhere, the Godly folks of Annapolis go to church. Respecting the Lord's day, he heads towards the towns' places of worship. There is almost one on each square. Throughout the morning, Clyde stops at each place of worship for an earnest moment of reflection and prayer. Some even serve communion wine. Perhaps Clyde should have restrained his devotion.

Attempting to bar the devout from each place of God there is a demon. It hopes to deter whoever they can drive from the Lord. Temptation takes the form of a different vice in each. Clyde resists each in turn. And is ridiculed by every demon. At the very last great house of worship he feels his heart stop completely as the bell in the tower tolls noon. Suddenly Clyde feels extremely thirsty.

From the moment their boat left the dock Christie and Dr. Ted knew they were on course. Even though the specific route wasn't recorded with favorable tide and current they are at the same spot just over the island.

This time, they each have two full tanks of air. With little effort they find the gap in the submerged hillside. It's precisely where they saw the terrapin disappear during their earlier trip. With air to spare they twist themselves through the entrance and onto a manmade rock shelf. It is where Christie spent so much time with Clyde's ghost. Being here she is certain Dr. Ted isn't the man she loves. She longs for Clyde but will settle for treasure. She lifts up her dive mask; he eyes go for the diamonds and gold. Christie has the fever.

They pick their way through the treasure judicially. The faint glow from their underwater lights guide their way. Christy immediately clutches an object she wants to carry away on this dive. She says, *"Ted, another day another dive; let's not sink our boat."* She manages to gather a few gems onto the boat. They wisely leave an innocuous marker at the entrance.

On some level they hope not to have collected any loot bearing a curse. But, there aren't "this is cursed" warnings posted. and any object they touch can be like a ticking bomb. As Hunter could attest, if he were here, curses don't carry hazard warnings.

Christie and Dr. Ted are Finished with their picking. Without talking, they hoist their muddy anchor. It drags a bit tearing up their underwater cave marker. They set course for the dock in Annapolis. They have disguised their treasure by using coolers. Belatedly Dr. Ted sees a DNR officer checking coolers on other boats for undersized rockfish. But he doesn't look in theirs upon seeing their struggle to carry these heavy ones.

After loading the coolers in Ted's trunk, they move their treasure back to her house in Annapolis. He moves to embrace Christie. Rather than a kiss or hug, she shakes his hand in a businesslike manner and smiles coldly. He shrugs, *"Well done."* She merely nods; then carries her share into the house without his help.

These two will quietly convert the jewelry into cash then deposits into bank accounts. They hope to salvage more in the future without setting off a modern day goldrush. Angel Ralph watches and realizes they are wise. Even when he imparts the realization to Clyde, the young man is unfazed. Clyde is happy for Christie. And all of this visiting, praying, and sipping has oblivious to everything.

For on this day of our Lord, Clyde decides he is finished with this world and prays to return to heaven. He fantasizes St. Peter and even the Lord will completely agree. Dreamily he decides once Christie hears her young beau is found prostrate before the altar, his life expired, she will shed a single teardrop of sorrow. Then have a divine moment of empathy.

Clyde sits in the empty church and sips quenching his thirst. He imagines, *"For at exactly noon today, while she and her treasure hunting partner are still inside of the cave, their lights will go out... At one minute past, the old torch on the wall will flicker and sputter then miraculously come alive lighting their way to safety."*

Clyde imagines himself transported back into the eternal light above unpretentiously. It's almost sneaky. There's no big ceremony or show. Gee simply takes him by the arm and tugs him. His new halo will be new and bright. Gee will explain to all, *"Clyde has earned heavens' highest mansion through his enduring virtue in the face of ungodly temptation."*

Clyde's going to be sad to think of never returning to the Chesapeake Bay area. *"For, I was Chesapeake born."* He thinks he's dizzy from the trip to heaven. He raves on, *'My new place in the ultimate domain is bright and fresh."* While his previous estate was also heaven this new position will be the best. But there's no tacky heaven. Saint Peter, the gatekeeper will usher him in will saying- *"Welcome to God's home in heaven!"*

Clyde's heavenly fantasy is interrupted. Far away he hears the voice of God saying- *"You aren't the keeper of my pearly gates; Peter is..."* Thud! he senses the painful shockwave as he crashes onto the marble floor of the last church he visited.

Moments later, Clyde's eyes open to the raspy voice of a cleric with a tall black hat saying, *"Mister, you can't sleep one the floor here; this is a church..."* Clyde hiccups.

"Also, you must repay the church for the cost of that ouzo." Clyde protests, *"I didn't touch your ouzo!"* The cleric points to the half empty ouzo bottle Clyde is using as a pillow. Clyde moans, *"I've been framed!"* The towering figure corrects Clyde, *"No son, you haven't been framed; you are pickled!"* Clyde realizes some strange forces have put him in this position and reaches for his wallet. Clyde hands the man a

bill sufficient to pay for a whole case of Greece's most formidable beverage. Sarcastically he points out while holding his head, *"This obviously is a house of God, but this sure ain't heaven."*

Clyde finds his way through a maze of winding streets and alleys. Back to the room he rents from Christie. He has little memory of Sunday before the moment he woke up on the church floor.

Christy arrives shortly carrying a cooler but without her treasure hunting partner. She takes one look at him and says, *"You look like you've aged ten years since this morning,...What happened?"* He looks in his wallet; his age is now clearly shown as 27. Clyde is more suitable to have a 22 year old girlfriend.

From this moment on she will have no memory of Clyde flirting with those sexy ladies of Main Street Annapolis. Their new reality is synchronized. And Clyde can only think, *"No more oyster shooters and no more ouzo." "I promise Lord!"* St. Peter just laughs out loud. *"They always think they've invented something new." "Jesus and the rest of us thought we invented oysters!" "Come to think of it, maybe He did!"* Then, asking another apostle, *"Hey Paul, did we have vodka back then."* A muffled voice answers, *"No vodka!"*

13

WALLOW

Once again the Lord orders the grim reaper to perform a difficult task. Gee needs help as usual. The last order, to remove all pirate ghosts from the Chesapeake actually saved Clyde's soul. This time his mandate is to quell the violence of Wallow's residents. It's been a giant slum without saving grace. Extreme punishment isn't an option because they do not understand right from wrong.

Obliterating Wallow completely with fire and brimstone would be easy. The destruction of the ancient cities of Sodom and Gomorrah was the right remedy for specific reason at that particular time. Even so there was the collateral damage to Lott's wife and daughters. *"If we turned every curious woman to salt today we'd run out of women within a week." "And those stupid daughters...whew!"* Rather than go through that insanity again, Gee decides to ask everyone he's helped in the vicinity of Wallow to help form a special committee to deal with his problem.

Gee selects a committee. The thought of having this loose bunch including Ralph, Lucien, Roman, Morris the zombie chauffer and even Teacher at one table is dicey. Gee has Morris pull them together in the backroom of an Elks Lodge near Glen Burnie.

He picked that town because to get anywhere in the modern world it's necessary to pass near the town. For a millennium people have passed through without the slightest idea they were in Glen Burnie. That's how friendly its' ghosts are. Not so a short distance away with aptly named Jumpers Hole.

Those who once were alive sit on one side; those from the hidden dimension are on the other. Zombie, Morris wouldn't sit on either side. So he sits at the end of the table. His job is to interpret where it is necessary. Always concerned about his appearance, Morris wears a newly acquired black uniform. Gee tells him to remove his cap; he does.

The only one utterly confused is Morris himself. No one ever got around to letting him know he isn't quite alive. Even so, So Morris usually just listens and says little. When Gee calls the meeting to order, they all become hushed. Gee opens the meeting with a prayer.

Oh Lord, please give us the grace to make

Your world a place of peace and happiness.

All say Amen including Clyde, who for some reason can hear Gee. Even though Clyde isn't here and doesn't know why. Then the grim reaper announces- *"You have been asked to come here today because we need your help to try to save a large distressed population."* Poor Clyde is completely confused but doesn't say anything because he's curious and wants to know what's going on.

"Because most of you don't know one another, I am assigning you positions on this committee." "Once you get underway, I will remain as honorary chairman." "To give you some idea of who one another are, I will start out by introducing Clyde, who wasn't invited and isn't here."

"Clyde has the distinction of having lived in two centuries: in three dimensions, and both on heaven and earth." *'And he just days ago, experienced a one day time warp that aged him by 10 years."*

"Clyde will serve as your presiding president." "Let's hear a cheer for Clyde." A condescending pause for a barely perceptible applause. Gee continues, *"I have also selected a vice-president; it's Morris, who some of you know." "Morris has a background particularly suited to Wallow's situation.*

"Morris is a former Air Force Policeman; he also served on a local police force." "And of course, Morris is our only zombie." The Committee applauds vigorously. *"Morris's experiences will be of great help to us..."* More applause... *Morris will conduct all meetings; Clyde won't be here but will listen and mentor as needed."*

"Our director in charge of demonic destruction is of course Ralph." "As some of you know, Ralph and Clyde were instrumental in rescuing an innocent girl and crushing the pirate ghosts who instigated her kidnapping."

More applause... *"And we have Roman." "He is my strongest analyst and will be a source of muscle if needed." "Dog and Roman will work as a team." "The rest of you will be ready reserve as needed." "We will meet again in one week." "This meeting is adjourned; thank you for volunteering."*

Clyde stifles an impulse to yell, *"What in hell have I volunteered to do?" "Oh, one final thing, you must not talk to Clyde if you see him; he's a mortal again" "We don't want people to think he's talking to himself."*

Dog would have run away from home if he knew what is about to happen. After all retrievers are bred to be work dogs, so he will follow orders. And this is the fate of all good work dogs. And that's a shame because the task at hand is hard.

As they depart, some mild comments of accord are heard... They agree to find every possible way to lessen Wallow residents' inclination to murder one another. Gee thinks, *"Why do people murder who must know that their turn to be killed will come?"*

First they will reset the clock of doom. To reboot it they will press the Wallow City Council to return prayer to public schools. As one agreeable city council member puts it, *"Saying prayers in school doesn't take any money out of my pocket."*

Others quickly agree and issue a press release- *The Commandments given to Mosses will be taught and followed.* The committee is determined do everything possible to save Wallow from itself. This move establishes a sense of reform even though no one on the council or in Wallow remembers any of the Commandments. It just sounds good.

Clyde has a lot on his plate for an individual whose mind was born in the much simpler era of the 19th century. He has set his goal to save Wallow through the Committee. But he really is on standby and his pursuits are in Annapolis. Sly old Gee involves Clyde so this will look good when he tries to get back into heaven.

On a romantic level, poor confused Christie must become acquainted with him as a more mature suitor. His recent time bending experience leaves him considerably more mature than Christie. Unexpectedly she notices a distinguished touch of grey in his sideburns. This attractive pair strolls smugly to lunch down Main Street. This time she is the exclusive object of his attention rather than those lovely ladies they pass. Even though some openly flirt with him. He remains aloof. Clyde only has eyes for her.

The fog in Clyde's mind has lifted about the days when he and a spirit, now called Ralph, saved Christie. Then vanquishing pirate ghosts languishing in the Chesapeake. He welcomes working with his sidekick Ralph once again. Even if it's only on the Wallow project. It doesn't bother Gee that Clyde has never seen a city larger than quaint little Annapolis. He hasn't even been to Buzzardville.

As their mentor, Clyde suggests several pairings and tactical operations. He suggests teaming Teachers' ghost with Ralph. Hopefully, with Teachers high degree of practice verbally jousting with Preacher and Ralph's muscle, they will persuade some of the more energetic Wallow ministers to emphasize the *"Thou shall not murder."* mandate.

Clyde refocuses on Christie. To be a husband and provider, he needs a way to earn a living so he can ask here for her hand in marriage. Christie and Clyde discuss what he might do for a living. He has business cards printed stating he is a certified appraiser of antiquities. It has a line reading- *Uniquely qualified*. Hopefully, no one will ask why.

Decades spent with pirate booty has given him the skill to spot reproductions and even fake antiques. Valuation isn't hard either. Christie is willing to help him keep up with how much people are willing to pay for paintings, coins, and other collectables. Cautiously they agree neither will research old wines. Hearing their thoughts, Ralph tells Lucien, *"That won't happen; wine to them is their snake in the grass."*

Ralph and Lucien are happy. Those two young people are coming together; and so is the couple in their house. But it's obvious to the angels for Christie's, mortal state she can't deal directly with immortals. Lucien suggests, *"Maybe we can arrange for Angela and Hiker to become their friends."*

Both couples are socially isolated and have many things in common. Lucien suggests it to Ralph, but he feels for now everyone has enough on their minds without even more complications. Reluctantly Lucien acquiesces... *"at least for now."*

Nevertheless, Lucien feels a need to work more closely with her newest avian apprentice as well as Dog. She arranges for Dog's spirit to take a sabbatical from the living animal. He is ordered help Roman to completely destroy the demon who wants to destroy Grace and her sons.

This is done as matter of factly as though the retriever is being ordered to fetch another duck. So Dog and Ralph are working on two projects at once. Ralph worries, *"It's one thing to send an angel but poor Dog is living flesh and blood!"*

Lucien sees Ralph's point, but her solution worries him just as much. *"Bird will stay at home to regulate Dog's normal physical functions while Dog's spirit chases after Buck's."* While Dog's spirit can be recharged with energy, Buck's evil echo spirit can't. On that miserable day Buck was ripped apart by Dog as he and two others were beating and robbing Hiker. Dog saved Hiker's life that day.

Dogs' spirit assumes the role of the Buck demons' worst nightmare. As it did on the day he rescued Hiker, it attacks Buck as a monster. Dog bites and tears at the demon.

Although it quickly returns to shape, it escapes in panic. It burns some of the limited amount of energy it has and will ever have. The pursuit is so swift and twisting; neither angel nor demon can follow the chase.

The dog spirit treed Buck's as it lurks by a spring. One that provides the only source water for Grace and her family to drink. True to his evil nature in life, Buck hopes to ensnare her beautiful soul. He quickly is flushed from this ignoble endeavor and is once more hunted rather than hunter.

Ghosts from the Carolinas and north to New York wager on the exact moment in time the spirit will run the demon to oblivion. Meantime, back in Elkridge, a raven enjoys his physical embodiment of Dog as the craziest pooch in the county. Even flees are terrified of him. It loves being this seemingly robotic animal.

Angela and Hiker are so into their own lives they fail to notice how lethargic their dog has become. The house is looking great. Her present goal is to understand how her investments should perform. At dinner she tells Hiker, *"Our fixed rate instruments and other savings accounts are safe but don't produce much of a return."* Safety of principle is the reason her father triggered his securities portfolio move to them if were to pass. Hiker doesn't say much but realizes this is the first time he's heard *"Our.."* He realizes, *"She's thinks I'm a keeper."*

Angela is gradually disclosing the extent of their wealth to him. In turn, he's slowly dropping hints to her about his work. About things she has no reason to know other than sheer curiosity. Hiker has completed his training and has been assigned to classified work in an office near Fort George Meade. He admits to himself, *"Angela and I have a weird sort of synergism."* In their wildest imaginations. neither has the slightest inkling they are the targets of intrigue.

Ralph and Lucien aren't extremely focused on their humans. Just a week later the Wallow Committee meets in exactly the same hall. It's an old Elks Lodge with genial ghosts. As he did the week before, Morris sits at one end of the table. He calls the meeting to order saying, *"Due to other commitments, Gee, our chairman, cannot be here."* Ralph gives him a knowing look. Morris continues, *"Gee has asked me to conduct this meeting in his place. We are to provide him with the details of anything we have learned about Wallow City during the past week."* He pauses, *"...and when and what we propose."*

"Please tell us what you feel should happen to start this off." No one says anything, so Morris begins, *"A million people live in Wallow, so we need to break the city down into manageable sections."* Morris then project an image of the city separated into quadrants. But the quarters are uneven so as to each represent one-fourth of the population.

"I say we try something different with each one; hopefully, we'll hit on useful solutions." As none of the others has the slightest notion of what to do, they each build on Morris's idea.

Teacher proposes, *"We do not need so many recreational facilities."* *"What good does it do to produce athletes who can't read, write or speak properly?"* *"They also*

need to learn how to perform the math for occupational roles."
"They also need the skills necessary to rebuild crumbling infrastructure." "Why use so much public money for athletics when so few make it to professional sports." "The rest just die and rot on the vines of despair!" "Not everyone can be a star..." "We need training for the average person as well as for the exceptional.'

Because they can't destroy any wrongdoer directly, after discussing the pros and cons, all agree on four cultural objectives. Morris records: decrease violent stimulus; kick out demonic thugs and thieves of every ilk; get rid of open air drug market; temper attitudes. Morris feels enthusiasm building.

Morris tells them, *"Committee members will work as a team for all quadrants rather than compete with each other."* Everyone will work to make certain all quadrants succeed. And they will try to persuade humans and good angels to contribute to their success. But because humans thrive on competition there will be a small degree of competition with recognition.

Losing is to be the only punishment for any who honestly try yet fail.

At the third committee meeting the outcomes were discussed. Clyde states, *"All four of these goals have lowered the violence in their respective quadrants and should be used throughout greater Wallow." "However some tweaks in application should be considered."*

Erase - cruelty from media and games
Isolate - evil doers and reward the virtuous
Teach - right from wrong and good from bad
Pray - raise consciousness of the Word of God
Learn - self-control and tolerance of others

By the fourth, the committee completes and submits their game plan to Gee. No feedback has been received from Gee since then. Morris reveals preliminary observations to the committee, *"We haven't reformed anyone entirely, but we have most of the worst wondering if their world is ending." "And most who despaired now look to the future with both hope and optimism."*

Teacher states emphatically that if we follow through with the ideas within this report we can accomplish exactly the things Gee needs to justify the survival of Wallow...and perhaps even other Wallows of this world. Not to relinquish his role as their mentor, Clyde's soul screams out to them in phrases he remembers from his maritime youth, *"Haul up the mainsail; set course you land lubbers!"* As a group they sing back, *"Aye Captain!"* At this moment Clyde and Christie happen to be together. She asks if he's losing his mind.

Trying to change the subject, she reads an ad to him from the Capital Gazette asking for bids on aspects of public works projects in Wallow City. She circles the ad. He promises to call a friend in the morning. He kneels on one knee and in a very traditional manner asks, *"Christie, may I have your hand in marriage.* She pauses, smiles, and says just one word. *"Yes!"*

14

SOUTHEAST QUAD

"We need an angel to finance the costs associated with the renewal of Wallow," Teacher reminds them. *"You angels don't have any money and normally don't need any,"* Lucien

pouts. Then a light goes on in his mind as Ralph points out the obvious business angel. One with no celestial title.

Angela has absolutely no experience with business wheeling and dealing. Even though she has inherited billions stashed away in multiple banks. This allows her to be easily influenced by her angel. Lucien presses her unconscious mind into believing financing new development in Wallow is a "great investment."

Lucien is not intentionally misleading Angela; she's just using the word *great* in terms of the positive benefit to the community. Truly sophisticated investors would quake at the thought of investing in Wallow as it is now. Ralph tries to reason with Lucien, but she has made up her mind.

Lucien has something those sophisticates don't, angel power. A slick young man, who just happens to be Clyde, calls on Angela shortly after her husband is dropped off at their home from work. Any negative opinion of Clyde's presentation of a theme park in Wallow is quickly brushed aside with a bit of help from Ralph. Any natural sense of good business passed down to him by Will Gold has disappeared in Lucien's embrace.

Clyde senses his old friend Ralph is in the big drawing room, but Hiker doesn't. Dog just lays at the foot of Hiker's chair giving both a belligerent stare and an occasional confused whine. Hiker says- *"Maybe he has to go outside."* Angela replies, *"If he does, you know he's perfectly capable of unlocking and turning the doorknob himself."* Clyde doesn't even blink wondering why this person doesn't realize the bizarre nature of what she has just said.

Clyde represents himself honestly as an antiquities expert and a volunteer for a committee to restore Wallow. And states he represents a group of concerned citizens dedicated to bringing an early American theme park to a distressed area as the first element of an urban renewal of the entire city. Both human investors nod in complete agreement with the idea. Angela cautiously asks for more details. Dog seems interested.

Clyde is thrilled at the ease of this monetary extraction. But rather than admit to Angela her money is the only financing the committee has come up with he manages to look mysterious and serious at the same time. He says, *"I will ask my partners to consider you as an investor if you will give me some idea as to the extent of your participation?"* She quickly replies to her husbands' chagrin, *"Whatever it takes."*

Ralph nods to Clyde telepathically, *"Clyde take a win and beat feet!"* Clyde stands and bows his head slightly to Angela and then to Hiker. He stammers, *"I promise to get back to you with more information within a week." "I must discuss this with my committee." "Thank you for allowing me to explain this with you."* Dog gags as if dislodging a furball then smacks his nose with his paw. *"This fool thinks he's a salesman." "She practically stuffed money into his pockets and this jackass puts her off until he discusses it with the committee." "He never was cut out to be a pirate!"*

Teacher has been bored ever since his pal Preacher flew off to glory land. He is assigned to research and quickly report back to the committee the process of 3D printing. Their museum needs objects of interest. Clyde tells Ralph he wants to replicate everything in plastic models from this areas' early American culture. Angela is funding the entire project.

Next, to get rid of southeast Wallow's residents who are mostly squatting in rundown or otherwise vacant houses with absentee owners. That is done rapidly by encouraging a blitz of housing inspectors. A few have been milking absentee landlords for bribes threatening big repair orders. Eminent domain notices followed by purchase contracts are mailed to the owners with simple postage paid return envelopes. Property moves into the program.

Clyde quickly visits the museums of nearby Washington, D.C. In several trips he copies nearly every interesting image of early Americana. Nearly everything except for the actual living pirates is reproduced in lifelike detail.

Bad teeth, scars, and all, he reproduces pirates he knew during his first lifetime. Someday, this historical display will be considered unique. No other record as detailed exists. Some scholars may claim this all false for it lacks the citation of source. Yet who, whose soul is purer than one of an angel or child, finds enchantment imagining spirits and ghosts? And whose else matters or cares?

The committee meets and fine tunes the process. Teacher prepares the final plan. When it's refined and Clyde presents it to Angela and Hiker it's an attractive investment prospectus. Even Dog wags his backend in a positive way. Angela went from being a passive housewife to becoming the areas' most wildly speculative real estate developer. All in only a day…with a lot of help from the angels.

Demolition cranes bash big and mighty balls against dirty brick walls. Huge shovels scoop up. Dump trucks come. When all is gone, dozers take it down to mother earth. And then it's naked as if nothing were ever here. The rats are dead; this land is clean and clear. And now it's done.

Crews of men and women from the other three Wallow quadrants come to build the new theme park. Pictures are taken at every point of progress. Someday they will point proudly to the magic they are completing. Since the project began, no one in Wallow was robbed, highjacked or murdered. As one might expect, not everyone displaced is content with the peace. Those thrive on strife and discontent.

Wallow opens without much fanfare except for a few media ads. This new theme park isn't far from other popular destinations. People have become bored with the present ones. Buses start rolling in from all directions. Wallow is a money magnet for other financiers. Upscale fast food chains buy out and level the old liquor stores.

Angela selects her own committee of experts to oversee matters of observance to theme. Clyde has guidance as he establishes the Board of businesspeople to run the company. He declines their offer to become chairman. He realizes, *"Chasing Christie was hard enough." "I'd rather walk the plank than run a business!"*

Of course many new employees are needed. A few come from as far away as Buzzardville. But they stay to themselves with the clear delusion they are of a superior culture. As one puts it, *"You can take me outa Buzzardville, but you can't take the buzzard out of me."* And all of the hidden dimension listen in awe and none understands why. Except that old Buzzardvillain just doesn't care.

Morris carefully selects a new security team. The city police have been great. Always short of personnel, Wallow's police have been enthusiastically helpful. Morris hires young military veterans are has them retrained. These are the most honest and serious minded mortals on earth.

Their community leadership supplants the four thugs as models for youth. Wallow has a new ethic of hard work and honesty. As one puts it, *"Working at the park means my mother doesn't have to spend all day on a bus coming to see me in jail."*

Several areas of the visitors center become classrooms at night when the day staff goes home. A consortium of four great colleges set up shop nearby for vets and residents. Angela and Hiker enroll. Angela enrolls in remedial math, Hiker takes cybersecurity.

Wallow quadrant southwest is needed to house new employees. Both quadrants northeast and northwest see a spike in property values. Gee's mandate from the Lord to reduce murder kicked off the whole process. His approach is given a favorable nod from above. The solution is so simple; the world just needs more angels.

Remember the shortcut Gee took when he tried to propel Clyde back into heaven without dying? Again forgiven, but certainly not forgotten. Especially by heavens' gatekeeper who growls- *"Definitely not forgotten!."* As always, the Grim Reaper walks on thin ice between both heaven and hell. St. Peter scoffs at Gee's suggestion he put a sign on the pearly gates- "No mortals allowed" Peter reminds Gee of resurrection day when the dead will rise.

Not every Wallow resident is happy with the new enterprise. Some were actually better off moneywise when the city was a lawless basket case. They profited from all types of vice and kickbacks. Then there are the perpetual malingerers.

Most feigned injury on the job. They continually receive underserved disability payments. This drains community funds and reduces the sum available to those genuinely injured and needy.

Degenerates who never have lived outside of Wallow miss the putrid bouquet of rotting garbage. For these connoisseurs of the phew, *"Fresh air doesn't smell like home."* The malcontents form a group they call SLUGS.

It's an acronym for - **S**ome **L**ike **U**s **G**ets **S**toned. Both thugs and SLUGS want little scrutiny. Both thrived in the murky places like old Lizard Alley. In Teacher's words, *"They are in dire need of detention."* Detention means considerably tougher justice to ex-cop Morris than to Teacher an educators' ghost.

Morris puts his foot down. When the committee meets he asks the group for authorization to form a special security task force. Replying to the question, *"What's wrong with the regular city police and the state troopers?"* As a former policeman he explains the laws are so watered down by a century of rulings favoring defense attorneys they are basically useless. The committee wants results; the task force listens.

Angela is asked for millions more for security and is happy to comply...but wonders- *"When does even the part I put in of my investment come back?"* Hiker jokes, *"Your reward will come in heaven."* She shrugs and wonders. *"Was I, am I good enough for heaven?"*

At first, the thugs saw this private police force to be no more a problem to them than shopping mall security. But this changes quickly as nonlethal injuries to thugs mounted. SLUGS experience less dramatic but as much trouble. Insurance Investigators can now safely track down disability cheaters with the protection of these supposed *mall cops.*

Evil demons are departing in terror as the new stocks are built. To human viewers only the wooden constraint is visible. But of course angels and demons within the hidden dimension see much more. Heads to tails, demons are padlocked in the stocks for all to ridicule. Demons torture demons because- *"It's what we demons do."*

For certain, the commandment *not to kill* only applies to living mortals. Therefor ghoul and demon slivers splash all over their dimension as the invisible task force chops them to hell. But they cannot and do not take one miserable life of even Wallow's worst thug.

Their living clients are about to face a treatment none have ever experienced. Resolution has come to Wallow. Nothing will be the same. From the stocks these demons cry out to warn their thugs *"They're coming to get you!"* In their final moments here the demons are telling the truth. Not one thug can even hear.

15

THUGS

Thugs are hard cases Morris hates. He must separate them from Wallow's most impressionable people. Having a thug shake them down for money. Even to force them to give up what little they own sets them back to zero. Without resources the victims become victimizers. This often leads to someone being murdered.

Teacher remembers being bullied and seeing others bullied both as young student and later as a teacher. Recalling those cowards and comparing them to these thugs, Teacher devises a systematic solution.

Morris's task force gets call data from city police records to develop statistics. They analyze crimes against the poor by quadrant to learn where most crime occurs. More importantly, which thugs are hurting this community the most.

Four stand out as kingpins. This quartet of thugs have terrorized their way into leadership positions. Several of them by battering and enslaving the weak. Particularly around lawless areas like Lizard Alley. The worst never gets his hands dirty. Morris will save him for last.

Teacher charts all challenges systematically. While Morris prefers a bare knuckle approach. Teacher begins with a graph by labeling the worst four thugs subject A, B and so on.

Morris patiently awaits his turn saying, *"When the rubber hits the road, I call a kick in their butts my end game."*

Because Morris is a zombie, whose police superiors thought had died in the line of duty, they never lifted his police powers. He still has a license. Morris can kill to protect the weak. Just the same he hasn't shown at his precinct for roll call for an awfully long time. In his mind he's taking some time off.

An early American saloon is replicated within the park and bears a close resemblance to one in early Wallow. It even serves food of the era and has a card game. Morris slides in through the swinging door and sits on a stool at the bar. A flowing spittoon of water passes between the stool and bar. Morris orders food and has a friendly conversation with the barkeep and swamper. A tough young thug comes up behind and says, *"Old man, you are about to buy a drink for me and my friends at the table."* To emphasize his threat he tips Morris's old cap off into the spittoon. Four pairs of eyes bore through seemingly poor old Morris.

Morris looks across the room. Two other thugs and a well dressed third are staring at Morris with a dare in their eyes." Morris demurs, *"Sorry, I was just leaving."* And is gone before anyone can move. His dry cap has returned to his head. But they haven't seen the last of this zombie. Morris grins to himself, *"They've just volunteered for the next stage of the cleanup of Wallow, but don't know it."*

Morris and the task force are reluctant to take human life, So Lucien is called in to use one her mesmerizing surges to daze the first thug. The nan is stunned. Making use of Gee's ability to move mortals, Subject A is transported to isolation. And suddenly finds himself on a unique island.

Over a hundred years ago, this island just outside of Baltimore is a hexagonally shaped fort designed to protect the city. It outlived its' purpose and was abandoned. Fort Carroll, a relic of a time when sailing ships were high tech, has been left decaying for nearly a century. It's mostly concrete and rusty iron. It's the perfect remedy for Subject A, a thug who needs victims. He is only victim here. There is no one left to bully on desolate Fort Carroll.

Just moments ago thug Subject A was drinking beer from a growler he got from Wallow Saloon. He's slouched in front of his TV. Teacher observes, *"Beer may give him hydration long enough to find water."* Morris asks, *"Is there water on this island?"* Teacher answers. *"I'm certain there must be water somewhere..."* He thinks he's just waking up from dozing. Morris thinks- *"He called me an old man, did he?"*

Oblivious to where he is, Subject A fumbles around in a stupor looking under rocks for his TV remote control. *"This show sucks!"* Teacher shrugs indifferently, *"We'll check back on him in a couple of days."* Hawk flies overhead trying to lead him to a clear puddle of rainwater. The raven reports to Teacher, *"He'll be more alert when he's dying of thirst."* *"No one can accuse us of killing him."*

Hearing this about A, his demon knows he has three days to complete his destruction. Imminent death is wonderful news to the devil. He ruminates, *"By then my demon could have this jerk end his own life in despair."* *"With his graceless life this loser will be with me in hell."* However once the Teacher and Morris have gone, the subject comes to his senses abruptly. At last he understands the gravity of his situation.

He looks around slowly increasingly conscious what he sees isn't on TV. It's real! That flickering purple mist on the horizon is Baltimore.. He is shocked to realize, *"I've been kidnapped!."* With no one in sight, he thinks, *"They're going to jump me as soon as I turn my back."* He takes out a blade and tries to intimidate whoever did this.

In the same mocking half laugh tone he used on Morris at Wallow Saloon, he yells at a concrete structure, *"Hey punk, get your sorry backside out here like a man!"* *"If you do, I might let you live."* No answer. He waits; still nothing. Subject A finally understands his dilemma. He's a bully with no one to bully. He's all alone. *"If you don't come out now I'm coming in there and you won't be able to come out!"*

"Oh my God!" Subject A realizes he's perched atop a high rock wall from which he can easily fall. *"I'll die if I fall down there.!"* His hand relaxes and the knife he was ready to cut someone with drops. Its' metal clanks sparking against the wall; it sinks beneath the bay. His blade is gone, his mind races.

First he thinks some other gang drugged and kidnapped him. Next he decides it was someone in his own gang and he's furious. He tries to figure out who did this. He is shocked to understand for the first time, *"all of them!"* *"They all hate my guts."* *"My buds put me here!"* *"Lord, please have mercy on my soul."*

The demon who constantly trails him senses disaster. It wants him to fall from this wall for his damned soul is a sure thing. It's an easy score. In spite of his hideous crimes up until this moment, Subject A prays without moving his lips, not even to breathe. Within a millisecond a splendid light obliterates his demon. Teacher and Morris wonder in awe, *"Who did that?"* Saint Peter shouts down to them, *"A higher power than mine!"*

"I was betting he would fall." He passes some grace to his buddy and gleefully asserts, *"I'm robbing Peter to pay Paul."*

Teacher is astounded, *"Who in hell ever thought Saint Peter has a sense of humor?"* Morris cautions- *"Not hell."* Teacher corrects himself, *"I meant, who in heaven?"* His oversight is overlooked by everyone in heaven, except for his old nemesis. Preacher keeps his amusement to himself for fear they'll be sent down. Shivering with rapture he remembers, *"Winters there are awfully cold."*

A celestial flash illuminates the hideous demon being as it brilliantly burns and falls from the wall into the frothy black water. But A remains unscathed.

Crabs are delighted to devour this garbage as they thrive on all things rotten. Subject A one may survive to find a pool of the nights' rain to drink tomorrow. But there's still the matter of what this thug will find to eat. And he can't catch crabs because his demonic bait is already theirs.

If Subject A eats the deadly toadstools, those that mimic mushrooms. The poison they hold will turn him to roadkill. Fine fare for vultures waiting just beyond his reach.

Graceful white gulls circle just above. Gulls screech wondering what this fool may consume. They flap over whether this wretch will only sicken or fully perish from the poison. Seeing little but toadstools, not one is willing to wager. Not a single feather is bet. Nary a gull wishes to be the bird brain. As for gulls, any game is a game with or without a wager.

Morris's task force doesn't wait for the fate of A. The destruction of his demon suggests for some reason he's been saved. If so, he's no longer a threat to the city. Subject B is next. Teacher sums up his existence. *"He's lousy with demons."* Subject A's vices supported only one. Gee asks, *"Why didn't you isolate B first?"* Teacher explains,

"Subject B has a following of sadists. Last week he and his cohorts hurt a man walking his old dog for the sick thrill of hearing them cry. His removal undeniably helps dissuade

others who saw him as a role model." He made the mistake of picking on Morris last week. Gee agrees with both choices. Most important though is no immortal has directly killed a mortal so far.

. Morris briefs the task force about the second thug. *"This character we list as B has the distinction of being the third worst thug in all of Wallow." "Subject A wasn't the worst." "We started with him to get our task force up to speed."* Lucien dazes Subject B just as they did subject A. The place of isolation where he regains his senses finds him standing alone in the dark. B's up his knees at the bottom of a smelly old well.

He regains consciousness in frigid water surrounded by natures' denizens who occupy this once pure source of water. They bump bite and crawl all over him as he swats, cusses and yells. This well was condemned because a septic tank is too close. Its' sewage trickles in. B stands in water that has been accumulating human waste for a long time. It smells like what it is. But its' nasty aroma doesn't bother snakes, slime and other critters who live here. In truth, Subject B doesn't mind the stench either for he rarely bathes. A degenerate lifestyle has buried both his body and soul to a level lower than the lowest slime within this putrid hole.

As with the previous subject, the ordeal B must cope with is converting accessible critters to food in order to keep from starving. Although disgusting, there's just enough water to survive. As for finding his way out of the slimy well, no human can hear him scream. Morris partially replaces the well cover. So it' s dark down here.

The teacher and task force are walking a fine line concerning their obligation not to kill any of these subjects. So they allow him to feel his cellphone. He retrieves it from his back pocket. B hasn't the slightest idea where he is. And the GPS is disabled. He calls his favorite number and orders a pizza with all of his favorite toppings. He waits for it to arrive.

Nearly an hour later it's delivered. But to the address on his account. This treat is gratefully received and devoured by one of his sycophants. As the days pass. B becomes so hungry he learns to munch on moss and swallow the water. Yet being only human he too pollutes the well. He decides he's in hell but isn't. He cries with more anguish than did the man with his old dog but senses no pain but his own and curses the Lord. This process could possibly change the way his mind works once his stomach settles. His dysentery is such that B will spend lots of time away from crime.

Teacher worries his death would be attributed to the task force and rationalizes, *"Eventually someone might stroll by and throw him a rope."* The committee decides that's too iffy. The next morning, the neighbors' dog observes the well cover, usually closed, is now partly open. It stands by the spot on the ground and barks relentlessly. After investigating the reason his dog is upset, the owner alerts the fire department. The thug applies for a job rebuilding Wallow. He now sees the world around himself as a survivor. One who appreciates life as only survivors can. Having felt so much pain he no longer causes it to others.

When old gang members want to know what's happening, B answers with, *"Cramps!"* It quickly gets around-*"B 's lost his mind."* This thug is no longer a role model. Now he's an object of pity. No one dares test him because of how dangerous he can be. B doesn't care; he joins the church and praises the Lord by singing in the choir.

The task force receives high praise for their work with the first two. They move on to the third with confidence. Subject C is conveyed to his exile in the same manner as the others. Teacher uses the isolation of C to amuse some of his former graveyard neighbors. This is to make up for his vociferous contentions with his old nemeses the Preacher. However, it is noted by the graveyard ghosts, *"The preacher is in heaven and that teacher ain't."* No one here among the ghosts knows the teacher decided to stay at least for now.

The third subject is carefully moved to an abandoned mill across from the churchyard. It's beneath old oaks across the road from the chapel. It's also where Hunter recently was liberated. This dilapidated mill is on the uphill side from the chapel just across the overgrown road. The once dynamic millstream is just a trickle. If C's lucky it will continue to keep him alive for however long he's here.

Subject C is invisibly tethered to a heavy round rock. The carved monster was the mills' wheel. His predicament might seem easier than that of the other subjects. The first two needed to find sustenance to survive. It would be easier except he is prone. C can only stand by lifting a massive chain. One only his eyes can see. He struggles, perspires, and profanes. Not one soul explains to him this chain is his depravity. His crimes weigh down his soul. It's so heavy but C cannot put down his burden. He doesn't pray to God; only his demons drive him ever on. He is true only to himself and to no one.

This spot is visited after the sun goes down by every animal of the woods. Bears and wolves watch him struggle, but they can't see those chains either. If they could they'd tear C apart and eat him alive. But they can't and see his struggles as just another humankind ploy to trap them.

Subject C was born in the city and lived as a bully. He must survive on whatever he can reach within the radius of his chain. He is so off of the beaten path, only hunters and mourners come by. It's a long time until hunting season and no one comes to mourn those who lay nearby. But, the way things are progressing in Buzzardville more may soon be buried over in the chapel cemetery.

Maybe C will be contrite when it happens? Who knows? The task force lets him live and so he will live on. No dog will bark; no raven will call. This man feels chained to a mighty millstone. A burden not real at all.

A Native American burial ground sits high over the place of C's burden. Here is the resting place of the sisters of Gin, mother to Vigilante Spirit. Her family hates thugs. A quick consultation with the ghost of Gin's sister elicits a promise to shield this thugs' predicament from sympathetic eyes. At this point Morris and Teacher are satisfied with the isolation of this subject. So they turn to the task of what to do with the last kingpin thug. Teacher refers to D as *Subject Death*.

While he is unquestionably a deadly thug, Subject Death is the most elusive. The first three were once SLUGS, this one is a criminal entrepreneur. His employees perform his murderous misdeeds. Many wouldn't believe he's evil even as they assist his crimes.

Subject Death's suit is immaculate, his hairstyle is sheer art, his custom shoes are masterpieces. He lives with his young trophy wife in a blinding showplace beaming from the glossiest covers of mansion and garden magazines. D's more slippery than any eel. Whenever confronted by authorities about his crimes, some poor stooge steps up to confess to anything his accusers might think to charge. Like the bloodsucker he is, Subject Death anesthetizes those whose life and blood he drains.

Death sits on prestigious boards and has membership in an expensive golf club. And he's a fundraiser for notable charities. While shunning political office himself, D supports politicians. Secretly he gives to both sides of the political spectrum. One committee member asks, *"Why was he selected?" "You've got the wrong guy!"* Morris turns to Teacher who compiled the list.. Always the academic. Teacher audits and divulges his research. He opens with, *"D isn't who he appears to be." "I've compared police reports, angelic observations of D's interactions with demonic associates and the flow of criminal activities over the past three years" "D's compound is the control center."*

Balancing his good to the community against this information, Teacher determines his *isolation* from the scene could save Wallow enough to finance a new medical center. The committee sanctions the move to isolate.

Following the committee vote to isolate, Morris reads the footnotes of Teacher's report to the committee.

> This subject is the largest corruptor of youth in the greater Wallow area. He is this areas' chief hard drug importer and distributor and his organization controls vice over a wide area with illegal activities in other major east coast cities.

Teacher continues, *"Authorities haven't been able to touch him because of his power base here." "This task force is uniquely capable of separating him from this base."*

The committee votes unanimously to do that very thing. No one suggests how. So, Death's destruction defaults to Morris. And, he's glad no one asks for details. They really don't want to know. If Morris does what needs to be done, after all as a zombie he's half mortal... *they hope.* They realize his task force is devious but offers them plausible deniability if anything goes wrong and *Death* actually dies.

Subject D is treated in a completely different manner because there's no hope for redemption. Isolating him with his demons in the way they did with the first three would empower his demons to rescue him. They want him to remain in power. Death is the devils' evil pawn. The worst of everything in the area begins with his organization. Gullible wanabees envy his way of life and desire to be just like him. They fail to understand his inability to enjoy the material things he has. Death's greed is insatiable.

Morris briefs his task force. *"We are not allowed to bump off D."* *"However, we must exorcise his goon squad of demons and disorganize his source of wealth."* Lucien points to the obvious,

"This is a job where we need Gee to not only convey but to overlook some of our methods." "But..." Ralph finishes for her, *"As guardians, we cannot condone taking the life of a human being." "But we aren't supposed to interfere with Gee's directive either."* She just sighs.

Lucien tells Ralph, *"Go see how the first three are coming along."* He reports back, *"Subject A is off of the island." "He tried to swim to shore but was rescued by a foreign vessel." "They convinced him to fill in for a crew member who quit." "Hawk say A's happy to leave his thuggish lifestyle for good."* They say out loud, *"For the good of Wallow."*

"Subjects B and C's isolation has been a success." "They have been neutralized and pose no further threat to this community." Ralph smiles and thinks, *"And no further threat to Angela's investment either."* Lucien playfully beams her husband over the spot where Lizard Alley once was. He bounces back to her. He likes the way it is now.

Although he isn't with the task force, Gee worries to himself about the mortality of Subject D. Gee knows Morris is going to stop D by fair means or foul with minimal adherence to the no kill rule. He starts by looking at D's normal life expectancy... In other words, how much longer can D be expected to live. The answer is disheartening. He has at least 20 more years unless he has an accident. He consoles himself with the argument criminals have a much shorter expectancy.

Hawk is beady eyed excited at the prospect of watching D's isolation unfold. The raven circles and reports the location of D and his men to Morris. *"Death has left the safety of his compound!"* *"But he's not alone."* The fact he isn't alone means it is not possible to transport him as he did A, B and C.

Once again the committee warns the task force, *"We are not allowed to kill him ourselves!"* *"Any of his stooges, or another human being with just cause, must do the deed."* They stop to wonder just who might do it... A name lights up in the Morris's mind. *"Sherriff McPherson!"* The man who shot poor Hunter down by mistake. McPherson eyes are better since his cataract operation and he has the fastest draw around. Morris rationalizes, *"Uh-h in self-defense of course and within his jurisdiction."*

In Buzzardville, today as usual, not much is going on. But if anything did happen or is going to happen old Sherriff "Mac" knows. Right now something he's being told bothers this old lawman.

The sheriff is worried when his deputy says to him, *"Boss, my nephew Wille was sure to get that convenience store just outside of town. Then outsiders came in an made a last minute offer the poor widow couldn't turn down." "Strangers gave her double what the old run down store is worth." "There's no way the bank would finance that much." "It would take forever for any honest business in that condition way out there just to break even!"*

The obvious question- why would the nephew even want it if it is so bad- remains unspoken. As both the sheriff and deputy know, the nephew has a lot of friends who hunt out of season. Buzzardville tolerates poaching game by hungry town folks, but never illegal drugs. Although the name of the stranger is unspoken both know the man Teacher calls Death.

The sheriffs' brow wrinkles. He orders, *"Take over here, I'm going to do some poking around."* The deputy looks at the rack of bulletproof vests. *"Yes I'm putting it one!."* The old lawman puts on his new bulletproof vest and then a lighter jacket. It's one that covers his badge. On the way out of back door he selects an antique cane from the locked cabinet. It's remarkably heavy for a walking stick. But the weight doesn't seem to bother him as he grips its' handle.

McPherson senses something ominous ahead. It's taken him nearly an hour to get here. Even so, he's not in a hurry. The sheriff turns off of the right side of the road into a picnic area. He's about 50 yards from the vacant store. His new dashcam starts recording. It documents each calm step he takes down a thin trail passing just behind the store. He walks as taking a stroll with eyes hidden behind dark glasses. A baseball cap shades his face. Still plodding along he holds his cane slightly above the weeds in front his feet.

Turning from the path into the side of the moldy white block building it becomes obvious he's being seen through the lens of at least two new security cameras. His neck hair bristles; instincts scream out danger! His left hand tightens the middle of the cane.

As he rounds the corner, an SUV with its' back hatch being slammed shut is before him. Two completely motionless men glare at him. Stealthily the lawman's right hand loosens the hand grip on the walking stick. A faint click… his finger sense assures him it's locked. He observes their AR-15s, while he appears unarmed. They pretend to be cordial as they tilt their rifles up to line up their shots.

As he passes, one of the men says, *"We aren't open yet…Mr. law man!"* The sheriff clears his throat, smiling graciously. McPherson turns and fires two shots…. from his walking stick. Subject D and his bodyguard collapse on the parking lot. Death's invisible demon is flabbergasted. After review, the bodyguard has homicide charges pending from a different jurisdiction. And Subject D's SUV contains a wide variety of illegal substances.

The inspection of the sheriff's' dashcam tape is performed by another cousin. He reports Sheriff Mac's dashcam was slightly out of focus towards the end. However it clearly shows the men reaching for weapons just before shots were fired.

Security cameras on the building did not survive the fire and so the only corroboration of Sheriff McPherson's report is the dashcam. But the two men were off to the side and out of view.

Perhaps any criminal charges made against the thug called Death wouldn't have been upheld upon appeal. Now with his death, no charges against Death or McPherson are necessary. As far as McPherson's quick trigger finger creating an inquiry, there isn't one living witnesses to dispute the sheriff's report. If there were, witnesses in the kingpins' world recant their testimony. And then, Subject D and his bodyguard went to the parking lot without telling anyone. Everyone around them believes they are on a trip. His organization is in chaos. And that's good for all who abide by the law.

Angels always know what demons are up to. No court of appeal operates within their dimension. It no longer matters who won when battles are done. The devil's happy with his share as the two thugs go there.

There's no redemption for these dead. St. Peter's side lost this battle. Nothing's left of these two souls to save or salvage. This skirmish is over; the battle is both won and lost. Morris's task force is satisfied Subject Death is gone. Gee reports to his superior, *"Three out of four isn't bad!"* *"That's 75 percent compared to the previous 5 percent."* As usual The Lord isn't taken in by Gee's hype. But He doesn't reign down fire and brimstone on Wallow either. Gee and the committee are satisfied.

Lovely Debbie, Death's young widow, will not believe he's deceased until he is declared dead some years later. Today she receives a loving text letting her know he's out of the country on business. Debbie is asked to temporarily fill his role with the charitable and civic committees. Lesser thugs were advised *"Don't talk to Debbie airhead; she ain't in da loop."* *"But do what she says, because she is your boss until I get back."* So, she's spared their nefarious side as they hunker down waiting for the bosses return.

She doesn't know anything about her husbands' evil business. They met after her first husband died. His brakes failed with a little help from the thug. D simply showed up in her life from out of the blue and provided consolation. She doesn't know what she would have done without him.

Buzzardville Fire Company didn't respond to the scene of the fire which destroyed the convenience store. They thought it's just over the line. So BFC reported it to what they thought was the appropriate county. But that county only has one engine and it is being used in a parade. Moreover they disagree about which side of the line the fire was on. It was actually on the Buzzardville side. BFC will respond to any future fires in the area according to fire chief McPherson, the sheriffs' brother by a different mother.

By the time a state fire marshal inspects the stone cold ashes there's nothing left of the store except grey cinders and black block walls. The state inspector solemnly reports the cause of the fire as probable rodent damage to wires. However he tells his wife he thinks someone torched it for the insurance money.

He senses arson because an accelerant was found. The fire marshal tries to contact the owner. But rather than state the cause of the blaze is arson, he deems it *"suspicious."*

The County clerk tells the fire marshal the buyer of the property isn't recorded on the deed. The buyers' widow says he was out of the country at the time of the blaze. She hasn't heard from him since he left and doesn't see any reason he would buy the place. *"Why would he need a place that far from everything?"* The sheriff knows why. If Death was caught he will deny any knowledge of his illegal activities here. The widow thought his purchase in cash was normal. Sheriff McPherson's nephew isn't so courteous as the settlement officer hands her a check for his purchase proceeds. Were she more educated, she wouldn't believe the first sale was just rent. *"I wish I knew more about business,"* as she buys her new condo.

The fire marshal notes, *"Any human remains at the scene would have been cremated."* The fire marshal spends an increasing amount of time hunting in the woods with his fourth cousin, the new buyer. The new buyer is the nephew who wanted it in the first place. The seller collected twice and doesn't know or care why she has so much money. And zombie Morris hums. *"...He's laid in the ground."* *"...He's laid in the ground."* *"Someday they'll all go down!"* Morris calls it his happy song. Teacher wonders when it will be time to tell Morris he's a zombie.

Crime in Wallow suffers a sharp blow with the loss of the nefarious four. Lesser thugs try to take the places of the first three. As usual gang warfare breaks out but settles down as the newbies become scared enough to leave town or murder one another vying to become kingpin.

Loser corpses are lifted out of Wallow and left for police to find elsewhere. The murder rate in nearby cities rises for a time. But Wallow enjoys a sharp drop in homicides and overall crime. Morris inspires the competition but doesn't kill anyone. Attrition and legitimate opportunity create a void among candidates of crime. Not a single stiff finds its' way to Buzzardville.

No one tries to replace Death. Only his kind and noble subterfuges survive him. Less formidable associates of the terrible four find rewarding careers within the new city. None looked back as did Lott's wife in the biblical account detailing the destruction of Sodom and Gomorrah. For now, none suffers her briny fate, but should they fail, sulfur and fire await.

Teacher proclaims to the committee, *"Honest labor rivals evil deeds."* Well above in heaven, his chum the preacher cheers, *"He's still spouting clichés!"* Saint Peter playfully smacks pious Preacher between his ears saying. *"Maybe in time you'll see him as you look up!"* Preacher pauses to adjust his hallo. Teacher replies. *"I'm looking up now and that old saint is not quite saintly."*

Sheriff's relation who lost the bid for the burned out store, pays a visit to Death's lonely widow. They met one another while both served on charitable committees. She mentions, *"I couldn't help but notice there's construction going on at the site where that ugly store burned down."* Then adds, *"My husband is still out of town." "We haven't spoken since he left." "Somehow I just know he'll never return."* She flashes her eyes invitingly.

"But you're welcome to stop by from time to time and perhaps catch up with him." He does "stop by" frequently and soon they become even more friendly. In due time she has her husband declared dead. Well before then, they will have developed a really great relationship. Understanding their missing boss better than most her husbands' old crew drifts away to places better suited to their talents. Sheriff McPherson sees to it in his happy *pick 'em all off one by one way.* *"Can't have no Deputy's nephew hanging with no trash."*

Gee praises the committee; he's satisfied their Wallow work is complete. Morris informs his task force it's dissolved. The Lord postpones reigning down fire and brimstone on the city until further notice. Gee warns the committee the future outlook for Wallow depends on how well people treat one another from now on.

With her cynical understanding of human nature, Lucien inspires Angela to take out a property insurance policy on the entire Wallow early American enterprise. *"One without a brimstone exclusion!"* Savoring his success with thugs, Teacher can't help himself when he says to the committee, *"All's well in Wallow."* But how can all be well when Wallow and elsewhere have clones running around?

Except for the things they don't know how to solve, Lucien and Ralph are extremely pleased with the progress. Remaining theme park pieces are gradually coming together. Yet that nagging clone worry hangs in the minds of all us here in the hidden dimension.

The worry, *"Who and why is someone sending clones?"* There are questions in Ralph's mind especially why isn't Lucien concerned? But he is wrong. Lucien simply trusts the answers will come when they are needed. Faith is the philosophy of believers. Lucien will soon have reason to treat this problem less philosophically. It's coming closer.

16

HARMLESS

Wars among this worlds' nations are of little concern to guardian angels. Beings of this ilk and dimension have no flag to favor in foreign affairs. Their interests are strictly dutiful in nature. And thus in this world of these angels, Ralph is the guardian angel of Hiker. As with all guardian angels around the world his charge is his main concern.

Hiker has typical earthly husband problems. No longer is he the carefree nature lover. Who could have guessed when he appeared on Angela's doorstep they would instantly fall in love.

Now Angela is pregnant. It's Hiker's job is to protect his growing family. In his fervor to be the provider, he's barely aware of Angela's inheritance, *"Angela and the children we have are my responsibility." "Anything her father left her isn't mine; it belongs to her." "Still, it's' good to know it's there."*

Roman moved on from being Hiker's guardian angel choosing instead to watch over Grace. She was the best of her lot. And She is a good mother. Even though she abandoned him to get away from his father who hated Mal. She belatedly renewed her motherhood with Hunter and has showered him with love. Both of her sons have a predisposition to drift into trouble the way Mal did with bad buddies. Even Hunter got into trouble because he refused to listen to the voice inside of his head telling him to be honest. Both are always restless. She confides to her friend after chapel, *"They get their trifling ways from their fathers' side."*

But their lot isn't Roman's problem. Like all grownups, their lives center around the routine. Reformed Mal has written a sermon for his mothers' next chapel service. The next time they go, Mal will limp down the aisle and ascend the pulpit. From that point of authority he will speak about, *"The prodigal son."* The pastor asked Mal to compose something he utterly understands. Roman smirks, *"He picked the right topic!"*

Hiker was overjoyed when she informed him he is to become a father. In a moment he may regret he promises to change diapers. Hating *eau de poop* as he calls it, Roman is glad he won't be around.

Dog doesn't mind the diaper idea though. Even Dumb ass became himself again once his spirit to his body and they came back together. Not so with the raven. Hawk misses being a dog so to amuse himself he barks at passing ghosts. Although ghosts like to frighten they don't like being startled and complain to Lucien. One threatens to pull every last feather from Hawk's jaded naked hide. Hawk settles for whistling opera. The songs birds hear are the songs birds sing. So if you're strolling along the Patapsco and imagine you hear Puccini coming from the trees… Who knows?

Angela calls upon her carpenters again. The same twins who spruced up the house. But this time to refurbish the bedroom next to theirs as a nursery. They show up with their wives for inspiration after Angela instructs them to- *"Just give it your best shot."* She hasn't the slightest idea about what should be in a nursery except her newborn. One of the wives crows, *"With eight kids between us… we are your nursery experts!"*

Dog entertains himself with corny musings like- *"I'm dog tired; I chased Buck's insipid spirit halfway to Buzzardville and back before he flamed out…"* He knows Raven would have praised him for his deed. Hawk just yawns. He sorely misses her and would really like to see her again. It's hopeless. Seraphim's and even the smartest dogs don't fall in love. And suppose they did; dogs really can't fly.

When Raven was incognito, posing as Lucien's assistant, things were different. Dumb ass was her best buddy as most dogs are. This raven they call Hawk thinks he's too important to sit around pecking the fat with a retriever. With his shiny beak and chrome black feathers Hawk's very aloof.

Strutting on the windowsill, Hawk admires his appearance in the glass. *"Feathers in place, both eyes looking straight ahead at the same time for once, beak sharp?" "No"* While admiring his reflection in the window he sharpens his beak on a weathered red brick. He puffs out his chest, sucks in a deep breath and takes to the air without a goodbye or go to hell.

Lucien has dispatched Hawk on a mission to the anatomy lab at the hospital in Baltimore. She wants some of the angels assigned there to volunteer for her pet project. Ralph would have gone if he weren't so busy keeping track of Hiker. He and Lucien are involved in serious work.

Hawk has no trouble locating guardian angel Michael and his anatomy lab cohorts. That is because about half are loafing on benches across from the lab in a small park. One's teasing butterflies. He puffs slightly beneath their wings just enough to lift them each time they alight on a blossom.

Mike is explaining why his angels remain to one of the Emergency Room angels. In truth the reason they watch over cadavers hasn't occurred here since the end of Prohibition. Cadavers no longer arrive in barrels of grain alcohol. It would not temp medical students of the present era. Yet rules change slowly in the hidden dimension. Hawk respectfully waits to speak. Mike pretends he can't see this intruder. It's the nature of this angel; he sees Hawk's conceit and puts him in his place.

As usual, Mike's guardian angels hover around the lab awaiting the final disposition of cadavers used to train medical students. Mostly those here in repose were assigned the same angels when alive. Just to help them understand the secrets beneath their skin. Guardian angels remain for good reason in this era of clones. In the distant past some corpses were defiled by other than the compassionate students. Although it hasn't happened at this Baltimore hospital, cadavers in some other labs were stolen for their parts to create clones.

At last Mike turns to this humbled raven, *"What do they call you?"* Mike asks. *"Hawk sir."* *What does your enlightener need of us sad guardians of saints?"* Hawk replies, *"Lucien inspired her charge Angela to invest in a business enterprise in Wallow."* Mike winces at the word.

"She needs everyone who can be spared to watch over the vulnerable workers there; some degenerates they call SLUGS are trying to exploit these without a protective buffer."

Mike is aghast. *"So, what Lucien and my friend Ralph want is for guardian angels to look after dozens of people instead of just one or two?"* Hawk croaks sheepishly- *"Yee ah!"*

Mike mischievously looks Hawk directly in the eyes crossing his eyes to compensate for the ravens' thin beak and says the most ridiculous thing ever to come out of an angel- *"Of course my associates require a hold harmless agreement."* Poor duped Hawk says sheepishly, *"Yes sir, I will convey your message." "You require a hold harmless agreement." "I will carry this information to Lucien right away!"* Mike says *"No, I want you to give the message to Ralph to deliver to Lucien." "Now, be on your way..."* Hawk flies back to the big house to report exactly as instructed.

Ralph listens carefully without expression. He approaches Lucien with mischief in his eyes smiling, *"Dear wife, if we didn't need Mike's help so badly, I would ask you to awaken a cadaver just to keep Mike's mind busy." "So, because we do need his help, can we pretend there is such a thing as a **hold harmless agreement** in this dimension?"*

He tries to determine where Mike got such an insane idea. A city ghost clues him in. *"Mike's been eavesdropping at the Law School around the corner from the hospital."* Ralph is shocked. *"You mean lawyers have guardian angels too?"* *"Yes, but don't tell anyone; they want to keep it a secret."* *"A couple even employ fallen angels too!"*

Lucien makes a quiet statement. One scarcely loud enough for just the nearest angels to hear. *"Once a year on All Saints Day, wake up one of their cadavers."* Mike, who is tuned in to her every thought rolls with joy on the hospital steps. *"Halloween is never going to be the same again!"* Just to be prudent though, he makes a quick trip around to the other teaching hospitals. His final stop, the city morgue.

Winging their way to Wallow, this mighty flight of angels stir the skies over BWI. Their crossing causes flights to stop for a night and a day. The official reason- lightning on the runway. When no reason is known, it's what they always say. The black feathered raven looks up to the heavens and flies with them in awe at this celestial armada.

As angels drop into Wallow City, Morris the zombie, assigns groups. SLUG's quickly find themselves overwhelmed. Morris is distracted from his guilt about how brutal the Buzzardville caper turned out. Then Gee warns him to be careful of slaying mortals.

Morris reminds Gee he is mortal. Gee doesn't argue. But he makes a mental note to sit down with Morris to explain he is actually only half alive. Morris just snickers to himself, *"They can't have it both ways."*

The committee hoped for something less final for the fourth subject than complete annihilation. However, the mans' bodyguard pointed his gun and was about to fire it at the sheriff. Crazier still, neither of the deceased thugs realized McPherson had a gun disguised as his walking stick.

Morris torments these worthless ghosts, *"Rest in peace losers!"* They vow revenge. Gee doesn't allow them to spin off echoes. Rather than allow them to create havoc, he express transits the ghost of the bodyguard to hell. Gee warns the dead kingpin, *"You're next."*

Subject Death's ghost crashes at the heavy wooden doors of a church begging for sanctuary. His imaginary fingers just can't grasp the brass door handle as he frantically tries to yank it open. Falling to his knees, his shapeless blob melts down grey steps and becomes loose in the gutter. Gee can't stop Death's soul from being snatched up by Death's clone.

Only a single clones' eye peers back from the slimy stream. It awaits the one who will collect it before it flows into putrid sewage treatment. Seeing his departure, the spirits of all the faithful departed in tombs beneath the church all whisper, *"Amen and good riddance."* But Gee knows better.

A yellow janitorial sign appears by the church steps with the customary red letters warning passing pedestrians - *"SLIPPERY WHEN WET."* But it doesn't appear Death's days are done for another clone will come. Because his soul is already in hell this clone has none. With no soul, he's just a common demon. One to be slain by all of any dimension. Morris decides to keep an eye on him for now. *"Let's see what he's up to."*

Their mighty new 3D printer reconstructs every structure of an early American town had except for the most obvious- the town saloon. For authenticity, Teacher and Roman put their imaginations together and come up with one that strangely resembles one that exploded. The very one that killed Teacher and Preacher.

The fragments in his mortal body left a lasting impression. As for Clyde, he never entered one back in his earlier lifetime which no doubt improved his prospects for sainthood. If he had he may not have made it to heaven.

Angela asks if anyone can provide some vague estimate of just how long it will take before some of her investment begins producing a return. They shamefully admit it will be a bit longer. It seems the public officials who have been running Wallow before construction are withholding permits while bluntly demanding kickbacks and favors for their major contributors. Only bad luck follows folly.

The Committee calls a special meeting to deal with the politicians. Once again Hawk is called on to fly over and get the goods on them. Except this time, the novice angel will also report to the area press. Of course no reporter is knowing going to accept a story from a bird. He will submit exposés from a whistle blower as a free-lance reporter. When asked how he wishes to be known, Hawk answers- *"The Beak on."* Of course the reporter thinks he's hearing something else. He reports his source as *"The Beacon."*

In fact if Hawk in his avian presence started to speak the scribe would have a stroke. So, this information is best thought of the Wallow version of *deep throat*. Hawk is a source who sends news releases perfectly edited for newsprint, or blog. The politicians freak out with paranoia.

The news media is promptly informed of all misdeeds regarding kickbacks. Bagmen are exposed. And soon Wallow's own media is forced to behave as a proper fourth estate. They finally dispatch inquiring reporters who are provided excellent editorial support. In the past most reporting on the obvious were forced out of their jobs.

Corrupt officials look everywhere for leaks except up at the assistant even leaves scraps on the windowsill of her office. They're for *"That cute little bird who always pecks at my window."* One morning he pecked at Angela and Hiker's window at an inappropriate moment in time for the newlyweds. Hawk now listens very carefully before he peeks. Now before pecking at their window he makes a show hopping around conspicuously. In birdlike manner he prunes himself, shakes his feathers and swears, *"No more dirty bird for the Hawk!"*

If he suspects anything is amiss in the bedroom, his vocal renditions are hard to overlook.

Back to Baltimore, the barmaid who suggested the big house to the burglars becomes tired of waiting for her cut of their haul. One afternoon another pair of Lizard Alley refugees stop in for a beer. She knows they're from Lizard Alley because it's the only place that smells worse than her place. She offers them the same deal as the first two…the ones who never got that far.

Cackling after they leave, *"Maybe this time I'll get lucky."* She won't because they aren't burglars, instead they'll wait around until she closes and take what they want from her till. For stealing her cashbox is the most these two could muster. Apprehended by two of Baltimore's best, under questioning they told everything she said, including her disappointment over the prior two she sent to be killed, bitten and maimed. In exchange for a lighter sentence, they tell all. She will be out of commission in a ball and chain facility for some time..

17

Musketeers

Although Hiker and Angela are awaiting their first child. Although they have a wonderful home life Angela had no relationship with doctors. Lucien inspired her to seek one. She did and now the very pregnant Angel is prepared to deliver when her moment arrives very soon. The nursery is ready, and Hiker is ready to take her to the hospital at a moment's notice.

Until a little one decides to show up Angela takes online business courses. She is naturally drawn to learning business. Hiker remarks, *"Why wouldn't you?" "You are Will Gold's flesh and blood." "You've inherited his mind for business."* Cautiously she begins investing the money her father put into her name. But in more profitable ventures than the regeneration of Wallow. Rather than becoming immersed in other risky businesses requiring her personal immersion, Angela studies and cautiously invests in mutual funds.

To offset her risky Wallow venture, she only buys into Morningstar's highest rated funds. She invests in most of the mutual funds of her father. The funds he moved out of when he knew he was about to die. Programed transfers were triggered just as poor Will was crashing into the rocks. With her new understanding of securities, Angela thinks some have become passé. She moves an equal amount of money into mutual funds each month using the dollar cost averaging strategy she learned from the lessons.

Angela doesn't visit the lake on the property; it spooks her. But this results in others trespassing. They totally ignore the old *Private Property- No Trespassing* signs. She senses something unholy about this cursed place. The place where her father died.

The return on the billions of dollars spread over these accounts has been dependable. Yet negligible due to low prevailing fixed interest rates. Her online courses occupy much of her days. After studying most mornings she prepares dinner and awaits her husband's arrival home from work each afternoon.

He works at a top secret government agency just about 15 miles from home. The eccentric group of thinkers in his section are all thinkers, not fighters. Their analytical minds mesh together well via their super computers. Ironically, the nature of their work requires every member of the group to qualify with a weapon once a year.

Except for Hiker, this bunch rarely sees the light of day. Their excuse, *"We read a lot."* When Hiker asks why, he's told, *"The guy who decided we have to qualify wasn't cleared to know what we actually do for a living." "Some of them think we're special forces, for others, it's flying saucers." "But, in reality we mostly sit and think." "Most other countries do the same thing; only no one else really knows." "That is except for each sides' paper warriors." "People rarely ever get hurt unless someone screws up." "Are you any good at solving puzzles?" "How are you with video games?" "No, don't worry, we'll teach you." "But first, get yourself to the firing range." "Don't worry, you'll pass." "No one here ever fails to qualify."* Hiker's brow wrinkles with worry he's going to be the agency's first failure to qualify with a rifle.

Down at the firing range, in turn he and his colleagues are told to lay prone and are warned not to shoot themselves. After popping a clip of bullets at the concentric circles of a target on the wall. He is sickened to see his target hasn't a single bullet hole he mumbles- *"How did I do?"* The instructor responds, *"You passed!"* Hiker confesses, *"But I missed the target."* The instructor comforts him in a condescending deep south voice, *"Son, you are only required to hit the wall, not necessarily the target." "If you're ever in battle, imagine how many of the other side's generals you'd hit by firing over their heads?"* The humor of it strikes them both funny. He leaves the range feeling better until the reality of his inept marksmanship sinks in.

Hiker realizes he needs to practice. Arriving home, he explains what happened to Angela. She tells him about a gun safe in the closet across from her fathers' desk. After an unusually quiet dinner she leads him to a dark musty corner. They come to an unlocked gun safe. She declares, *"I want to learn how to shoot too."* He agrees Angela must be able to protect herself while he is at work. After checking out the impressive and sizable collection of shotguns and rifles they withdraw from the late Will Gold's arsenal. Retiring to their bedroom, they resolve to begin marksmanship practice in the morning.

Hiker carries a bottle of Cabernet Sauvignon for himself, a bottle of water for Angela, plus a can of whipped cream. Dog likes whipped cream and wants some. He stealthily tries to follow them. He trails stealthily.

But Dog is abruptly blocked from the bedroom door. Because they slam the door leaving him staring at it blinking, *"Damn, I like whipped cream too."* *"Now it sounds like they're in there laughing at me!"* Lucien consoles him saying, *"Dog, sometimes it's just not about you!"* Dumb ass just licks his paw and scratches behind one ear. He dozes and woofs in his dreamy sleep. Both paws paddle the air furiously struggling to run somewhere after an imaginary something only dogs can see.

Just after midnight, a faint sound from the front door interrupts his canine fantasy. Abruptly this belittled pooch becomes fully alert. He charges full speed down the long staircase. The normal soft barking woof from his throat is once again a hysterical beastly roar. It's trying to warn, *"We are being attacked!" "Wake up, get up; somebody's breaking down the door...!"*

Still the sleeping lovers barely stir. Glass shatters. The intruders realize their element of surprise is lost. They batter the heavy door with all of their strength. As all hell breaks loose Angela and Hiker come alive. Both angels are screaming in terror. Hiker stumbles foggily into his trousers and shoes. Every nerve vibrates, his body quakes. The empty wine bottle rolls across the bedroom. But he is up and running.

Both guardian angels are at full alarm. Hawk is alert and awaiting orders. Still Hiker and Angela in the big master bedroom seem slow to respond. Finally hearing everything they stumble out of the bedroom door. Hiker races for the gun safe Angela disclosed just before they came to bed.

Running, stumbling back down the steps he almost falls over Angela. She's poised pistol raised and steady. Then she brushes past him running down the stairs. Hiker runs after her impressively waving a shotgun. The prowlers have smashed open the front door. The leading one wields a machete that he is slashes at their dog. At the top of his lungs, Hiker screams, *"Get away from here!"* Seeing only a dog and two half dressed people they keep attacking. The machete connects with the dog enraging him even more. The second has an old luger. But bloody dog throws him off balance. He can't level to aim. He pulls the trigger. Bullets spray all over the place but hit no one, not even the dog.

Although the dogs' shoulder suffers a long slash, his teeth have one intruder by the leg. Jaws grip; muscle and bone rips. Teeth holding fast, dog spins dodging a second chop of the blade trying to slash his head. Angel pulls the trigger and drops the one with the gun firing a single shot at his chest. An eerie whining terminal breath escapes him through the new notch in his lung. He lays dead on the floor.

For good measure, the dogs' powerful jaw snaps through his leg bone. His blood covers his corpse; his ghost erupts. It's whacked out of the house by Ralph. Just in case someone thinks he knocked off a living mortal, Ralph makes the situation clear. *"This robber was dead when I hit him."* *"Ghosts are fair game for angels!"* Ralph knows, everyone in the hidden dimension knows Ralph misses his vigilante days.

The remaining robber begs for mercy. Even so, Hiker tries to fire his empty shotgun. Failing to make it work, he clubs the remaining miscreant squarely between his ears using the overhead route. Both intruders are done. Regrettably, brave Dumb ass is a wounded bloody mess. But continues to cling to the disemboweled limb as though clutching a dead duck. He's ashamed to realize he enjoys biting bad people.

Angela recalls Hiker telling her, *"If anyone tries to hurt either of us call the duty officer at my work and not local police."* With a mental prod from Lucien, she runs directly to the table where Hiker left the number. A calm voice answers, *"Just stay calm; we'll be there quickly."* During his initial briefing at work it was explained. *"The Howard County police are completely trustworthy." "Some may not have the training to know how to secure classified materials they may find at our employees' crime or accident scene."*

By the time Angela wraps Hiker's feet, removes the broken glass from the door and ties a towel around Dog, two vehicles are silently coming up the driveway. The surviving burglar shivers violently in shock as he bleeds out onto her floor. She scornfully uses a towel to sweeps his spreading blood puddle back at him. His eyes are open wide but see naught. Angela resists the impulse to finish him off. Hiker makes coffee; His guardian angel Ralph hovers exhausted.

Angela and Lucien peer out from the splintered front door onto the long circular driveway. They watch an ominous fleet of black vehicles appear. One set of uniforms wrest the disemboweled leg from the weakly growling dogs' teeth. Then slide it into a zipper bag along with its' dead owner. They move the him into a black van and quietly drive away. Another two carry the second. He is barely alive but bandaged and shackled to a litter. A uniformed officer explains, *"The shackles are a precautionary measure."* But he's going nowhere, except to where they take him.

All exit as quickly as they had arrived. A neighbor in jogging clothes came in unnoticed with the first responders. Seeing the two laying in the glass, he informed the uniformed agent standing next to Angela he has seen these two parked out on the road several times over the past week. He assumed they were workmen.

The agent thanks the jogger but surprisingly doesn't ask his name. Then he says to Angela and Hiker, *"As a matter of national security please don't tell what you've seen here to anyone including your family as it could endanger you and your loved ones."* The jogger smiles saying. *"I'm going home now.* To the agent, *"You fellows know where to reach me if you need anything."* The agent nods and thanks him for his help.

The two return to bed and try to sleep. However, when morning sunlight shines into the room it finds the couple still wide awake. A slim nearly empty Cabernet bottle reflects the rays from its' black shiny sides with his straw still standing erect. A passing ghost observes, *"Nobody drinks wine with a straw."*

The empty bottle and the whipped cream can are the only signs of the happy moments they shared in last evenings hours before the confrontation. Poor Dog is off to an animal hospital to heal. He was too weak to pull off his stained towel. Just the sound of the raven on the windowsill can heard. It's inappropriately quiet as if nothing happened during the night. Ralph and Lucien are shaken. But Hawk flies off to see how the dog fares. He likes the dumb animal after all.

Questions race through Angela's mind. *"Why did I have a flashback in which I'm someone else?"* *"Who were those two people with us just before everyone arrived?"* *"Where did they go?"* *"Did my father show me how to shoot a gun?"* Finally the realization hits her…" She clutches Hiker. *"I *shot someone dead." "I actually took the life of another human being... God forgive me!"* Her husband finally dozes off barely hearing her. He thinks she's bugging him to go down and fix the front door. *"I'll do it in the morning dear." Just go to sleep"* Reassured after seeing Dumb ass's stitched Hawk sits in the doorway ready to stare down any ghost who might try to trespass.

There is nothing angels Lucien and Ralph can express to soothe her that Angela can hear. Instead, the raven now known as Hawk distracts her by pecking on her window. She goes downstairs for some breadcrumbs. By the time she gets back the bird has flown. She distracts herself by cleaning up broken glass and blood from the floor just inside of the door.

Next she calls the twins to fix the broken door glass and orders them to have a security alarm company to rig an alarm system. She can't stand the notion of being here all alone every day without something to prevent this from happening again.

In reality the couple are far from alone. If Angela were just to look out of her window she would observe armed men hiding behind bushes. Others in gully suits pretend to be a low string of brush just beyond an empty concrete pool. At just past noon, her husband jumps out of bed in a panic screaming, *"Oh my God, I'm so late for work, I am going to lose my job!"* Ralph laughs. *"For an intelligence analyst he's clueless."*

Several weeks pass: things are seemingly better. The FBI traces the history of the burglars. It decides they were simple garden variety criminals rather than a terrorist cell. After serious interrogation at the prison hospital the surviving burglar regains his wits enough to confess he was the cellmate of the deceased. After escaping from prison, they drifted from suburb to suburb ravaging large old homes; the kind that often have little security.

The agency sends a car for Hiker and Angela to pick up Dog from the animal hospital. On the way home he lets them know he needs to use a fireplug. The vet pumped so much fluid into Dog he will be raising his leg every hour for a week. They stop by the side of the river. The two humans sit on a bench and release the car. *"We'll walk the rest of the way home."*

Meanwhile Dog gingerly limps up and down by each bush relieving his bladder as well as everything else. He's sore.

Angela and Hiker had never picked up on the name his original master had used. *Dumb ass* was the name Hunter had called him and which the spirits and angels copied. Hiker tells Angela as Dog sits panting, *"You know Angie, we've never given our friend here a real name...we just call him Dog." "This is the second time he's come through for me...Dog here saved my life again last night."*

She agrees patting him gently. Dog's chest swells and he smiles. But they don't notice. She points out, *"We were just like the three musketeers." "We were one for all and all for one."* He nods looking at her. *"Do you remember who wrote that book?"* She replies, *"...The Three Musketeers themselves?" "No!"* He declares, *"Alexandre Dumas wrote The Three Musketeers."* She pretends to recall, *"That's right."* Pointing to their dog, Hiker announces to the world... *"Dog from now on your name is Dumas!"* Dog falls on his paws in shock.

He becomes so weak with the thought of becoming officially either Dumb ass, or Dumas. Much too weak to walk. They have to carry poor Dumas all of the way up the hill because the agency car had to leave. He whimpers, *"If they only knew how I hated being called Dumb ass." "Dumas is just the same."* Ralph gives him the stink eye, *"Oh yeah, you didn't need to enjoy chewing off that fools' leg so much either!"* Dumas reflects to himself, *"Well, it's better than polecat."*

While Angela and Hiker are rather relieved their home wasn't invaded by terrorists, their guardian angels worry. *"Maybe the culprits were guided by demons?"* Ralph asks Lucien which would be worse. Lucien shrugs, *"One is as bad as the other..." "There is no better." "Does it make it any better if a black bear kills someone or a grizzly?" "You're just as dead either way." "And what's going on with those clones?"* Lucien knows when they're around by the absence of ghosts. Ghosts are afraid of clones because in passing they become exponentially more powerful, even though the only have one soul.

She dispatches Hawk to survey the area. He returns with troubling news. *"Those ghosts who always hang out down by the Viaduct have moved."* This news is troubling because the once thriving Patapsco Valley has always had a large ghost population. Lucien directs him to look further to see where they might had gone. *"And ask why they left."* No ghost leaves their favorite haunt unless they have good reason. It's where their friends are; their haunt is their home.

Their homelife remains good after the shock of the home invasion passes. But Hiker has become increasing stressed by the responsibilities of his work at the agency. He is responsible to detect and report an increasing number of threats to the people of his country. By definition, his country includes everyone in the world, his loved ones at home and his estranged parents. They seldom are visited but are always in his heart. But that's a long story he keeps to himself.

Angela, although the love of his life remains a woman of mystery. *"How does someone who didn't know how to hold a pistol, an hour later, load one with the correct ammunition?"*

"Then with cool precision she blew away an intruder dead." *"OK, so her father either taught her or, she learned it somewhere else."* He admits to himself he might be dead if she didn't know those things.

He loves her and yet these questions nag him. *"What else does she know?"* His mind, one so valuable to his employer for its' analytic ability makes him miserable with questions he can't answer. *"Why do I have to know things?"*

That morning, an alarming photo crosses his desk. It's the face of a spy. In fact, a face of someone who was in his home. It's of his neighbor who seems to be constantly jogging. His intentions to tell Angela about the spy come to an abrupt halt when he arrives home to find the very same individual seated in his parlor discussing the break-in with Angela.

He enters the room to a pleasant greeting from both. The man stands to shake hands with Hiker. Angela introduces him as Jim Smith, *"He stopped by to see whether we have recovered from our ordeal."* Instantly, Hiker realizes this mans' name is far different than Smith. Instead he is Abdul, a foreign national of a middle eastern country. Hiker quickly excuses himself saying he needs to freshen up a bit.

Reaching their upstairs bathroom, Hiker runs the water, flushes the toilet, and calls the duty officer of his section at work. The officer tells Hiker to stall the man as long as possible. *"I'll have someone there within an hour; don't let on you know his identity."* Hiker joins his wife and the imposter asking in a cordial manner, *"What type of work are you in Mr. Smith?"* With only the most remote hint of accent, Mr. Smith says, *"Investments, what is it you do?"* Realizing this spy has seen everything that recently went on, including men with sniper rifles, Hiker blithely states, *"I work for a company that catches spies...like you Sir!"* Angel simply groans, as do Lucien and Ralph. Rather than wait for a response Hiker continues, *"We have been watching you for some time; obviously, are you here to seek asylum?"*

Their visitors' face displays an involuntary flash of irritation. Then very calmly he protests, *"Although I haven't the slightest idea what you are talking about, I am willing to* tolerate whatever you wish to say." Hiker rolls his eyes and says, *"I am not a negotiator." "I have a friend who should be here any minute. One who may be able to offer some information on the subject."* The jogger stands up saying, *"I do not plan to be here when your friend arrives!"* He smiles at Angela and leaves. Hiker is beside himself with frustration.

More than an hour later there is a knock on the front door. The man at the door has a harried expression. *"I am truly sorry; there was a pileup on 695."* Seeing Hiker's vapid expression, *"He's gone?"* Angela states, *"He's gone, but if you look over your shoulder and across the street you'll see he's taking your picture."* A week goes by; nothing is heard.

Then, one afternoon Hiker is informed by his supervisor the director wishes to see him in his office in the main building. This causes a stir in his section because none of his fellow analysts have ever been in close proximity of the big guy. His supervisor doesn't ask him what he's done or why. But his expression shows clear concern. It's a matter of need to know and his boss knows better than to ask. He can only hope Hiker will clue him in later.

A pool car with a driver waits at the gate. They pass through a maze of guarded gates until arriving at an underground parking entrance. They are screened remotely at each turn by lenses on every pole and nook.

Three uniformed guards inspect the cars' interior and beneath the chassis with mirrors and another device. Next they scan his eyeballs and hands. Seemingly verified to be authentic, Hiker is so stressed from all of this protocol. The young man can feel his knees knock as they ride up the elevator. It eventually stops and the door opens where two more guards join the three. Now he has five escorts. He wonders whether someone is worried he might steal a paperclip.

They escort him through a maze of cubicles and more doors to a second elevator. Along the way he feels appraising side glances from dozens of eyes. A cold chill grips his stomach as he worries what will happen if he tells his escorts he needs to use the men's room. Will they watch him?

This elevator moves smoothly without a floor indicator. At one point he senses it moving horizontally rather than up or down. The rear of the elevator opens. A slim waspish woman in a business suit crisply states, *"The Director expects you."* Three of their escorts turn and leave.

The woman opens the door to a small office and presses a button on the desk. A green indicator light blinks and the lock clicks open. They walk into a much larger thickly carpeted office with the requisite photograph of the *POTUS*. She asks, *"Would you care for coffee or tea?"* He replies, *"No thank you."* He decides he is being treated hospitably and thinks- *"That's a good sign." "At least he doesn't hate me."*

The Director has his back to them and is speaking quietly into a landline phone. Hiker stammers, *"Hello."* Hiker feels stupid. The Director ignores him and doesn't seem to have heard his rude intrusion. The woman motions for him to be seated. Hiker sits and breathes more calmly. She continues to wait standing. His stomach churns realizing his chair is lower than the Directors and his associate is hovering just behind his line of vision. *"Is she going to murder me?"*

The area in front of the desk where Hiker is seated is brightly lit while where the Director sits is shaded. Still engaged in his conversation the Director waves his hand; the woman and remaining escorts turn and leave. He is alone with one of the most powerful men in government.

Hiker stares anxiously at the shadowed figure. The phone conversation ends and the Director jumps to his feet, turns towards Hiker and shoves out his hand and pleasantly says, *"Welcome to the funny farm!"* *"I AM the real Jim Smith!"* *"The gentleman you met was my double."* *"We take turns jogging in the neighborhood."* *"That is why I always seem to be outside."*

Anticipating Hiker's question, *"Why did the FBI send a man to interview you at my place?"* The Director replies, *"You painted a picture of me; it's one we try to maintain."* *"The person you talked to on the phone has no reason to know who I really am." "The reason I feel it's necessary for you to know now is because you live so close to my home." "One of us would need to move or the other, just to keep you or your lovely wife from becoming overly patriotic and doing to me what you did to those burglars." "For mild mannered people, you too are a real menace!"*

Hiker finds himself amused. Then the Director reveals, *"You were very astute, the man you found sitting with Angela was an imposter." "We use him as my double." "He was given asylum here several years ago, so your offer was unnecessary."*

Smith continues. *"And, the reason we didn't ask your wife to come in today is because we haven't been able to complete her security clearance."* Hiker hides his shock that Angela needs a clearance. *"No one in the area remembers seeing her growing up in the neighborhood." "Isn't that a little bit odd?" "My double was trying to learn enough about her to complete her clearance when you tried to grant him asylum."*

Hiker explains the circumstances under which they met. *"I wandered in one day and we fell in love at first sight." Her father, the late William Gold, kept her pretty secluded from the world because of his personal wealth." "They each had terrible accidents at just about the same time." "Angela recovered from hers with no memory of her past." "We know of her upbringing pretty much from documents she's found in his files..."*

The Director looks at him strangely saying, *"We need a better cover for me." "I'll get back to you after we check things out further." "Do not tell anyone who I am, especially your neighbors...and that includes the people in your department." "Is that clear?"* It is easy for Hiker to agree because he's never spoken with any neighbor except Jim Smith.

"My identity is strictly on a need to know basis." Another being in the room also knows who the Director is... His guardian angel decides more than just neighbors memories need to be altered. The Director's observation is an

understatement. Angela obviously didn't grow up in the house of her father. Her mother raised her in filthy bar where she was exploited. Now Lucien will arrange a better history for her. All angels and demons and politicians know- *"Reality is whatever one believes regardless of fact."*

With the help of these angels, tonight the Director and Mrs. Smith will recall the spirited girl across the road who rode her sled down the hill every time it snowed. Hiker will recall his conversation with the Director where he was assured Angela's clearance although late is approved. In this revision, the Director has given him permission to let Angela know the man across the street isn't a spy. Lucien and Ralph prefer this reality. But it's not going to happen tonight. Unfortunately, there is an issue overlooked…this problem of clones. They get lost in the shuffle of memory revision. And this problem is about to become real.

As Hiker leaves his meeting, the Director's personal assistant awaits in the outer office explaining, *"Because it's so late the escorts are gone for the day; I'll walk you down to where your ride will pick you up."* There are no guards now. They proceed down a backway through the boiler room and its' maze of pipes going in every direction. They reach a point just behind a dumpster. He's surprised at this weird place. She turns and abruptly leaves without a word except to unclip and take back his visitors badge.

He supposes he has arrived at the spot where he is now to meet his driver. It surprises him that a far different vehicle stops because the driver told him he would pick him up where he left him off earlier. A red corvette pulls up; the driver of the car motions for him to get in. It appears to be Director Smith. Hiker thinks it very strange, but Smith is their boss and everything about this business seems designed to confuse.

Little conversation occurs between the two until they are far from the compound. Then the driver says, *"Nice weather today."* As Hiker nods and responds in agreement he realizes Smith's slight middle east hint of an accent is absent. It wasn't evident during their entire conversation this morning. Although Hiker's senses are on full alert, still nothing he says the rest of the way home would indicate danger. He believes he's once again with the Director's double thinking- *"This is some kind of a test to see how sharp I am."*

They carry on a normal conversation about sports. And it's obvious to Ralph, who is hovering behind them, neither knows much of anything he's talking about. Hiker watches the driver closely. Not far from home he realizes they have taken a wrong turn onto a forest access road designed for park vehicles. Without warning the driver turns abruptly into a hidden entrance to an opening in the hillside saying, *"Relax, this is a shortcut; we'll be home in a few minutes."* But Hiker quickly realizes they won't.

The doors into the base of the bridge might seem to be only for utility purposes. Most like this are but this one isn't. Moments later finds them speeding down a long dark wet tunnel. They were averaging 30 mph coming in. Now he would guesses they're up to 65. He realizes somehow he has been drugged. The driver has slipped on a gas mask, one that unfortunately blocks part of his vision. If he were conscious, which Hiker is no longer he'd be terrified.

Hiker's earlier pool car and its' driver pull up to the big house. Angela comes out to greet Hiker. The man who kisses her looks and sounds almost like her husband. Angela knows something's wrong but doesn't understand what. Lucien knows but can't tell. Angela has no idea what to do and has no way to realize she isn't alone with the imposter. Dumas knows and growls at the man eyeing up the man's leg and drooling.

While back in the tunnel the corvette hits a slippery spot. It flips over striking a post. Maybe Hiker's limp state saves him as they spin out and the car is splintered. The driver is torn apart. Hiker has scratches but the air bag on his side deployed at the moment of impact and didn't explode.. Hiker knows he must get out fast and put considerable distance between himself and the burning car.

His door opens and he rolls onto the concrete floor of the tunnel. An emergency notification system gets its' signal out as does his urgent text to Angela. She reads it and clearly understands she is face to face with an imposter. In fact he is her husbands' clone.

Hiker wonders why he's watching the Directors' double burn. There's obviously no appropriate first aid. He is stumbling away from an inferno in some abandoned storage building. The dead phony is toasted in his jogging clothes. But this obviously isn't the Directors double either. He decides there are too many damned Directors. Hiker tells the corpse across from him through bleary eyes. *"I feel like I've been drugged." "What's going on?"*

In perfect English, the ghost of the clone tells Hiker, *"You have." "You poor fool, at this very moment your other self is about to make love to your wife."* Apologetically he tells Hiker, *"You only have one chance to recover the life you've enjoyed up until this moment." "Otherwise he will permanently assume your life and become the father your child."* As the demons come for the clone he sarcastically sneers, *"He will take her to new heights of love she has never before known." "We know everything there is to know about your privileged little sweetheart."* But his threat is wasted. Then this one is gone leaving just two Directors for the time being.

Hiker cannot hear him as the clone ghost is dragged away it blanches and seems to upchuck. Ralph, the guardian angel looks at the ghost and mockingly asks- *"What can I do for you?"* The bodyless one shrieks, *"Tell me everything you have learned about me at the place where he works."* Then he screams in terror realizing the person he is extorting isn't Hiker and that his own body and the gas mask were incinerated.

Angela smiles very slyly asking Hiker's clone, *"Where have you been; why so late?"* The imposter replies, *"I had a meeting dear." "I'm so sorry!"* He brushes her lips with his thumb and kisses her. She's nauseous with the realization. *"This imposter thinks I'm going to act like his wife!"*

She understands no one will help her. But can't stand the idea of killing another human being. Her destruction of the intruder only last week still gnaws at her soul. Angela doesn't want to shoot and loosens her hand from the gun in her coat. So she does the next best thing.

She waits until the imposter to turn to hang up his coat. Instantly she grabs an iron from the fireplace and smashes him in back of his head. He falls to the floor like one of the ducks Dumas always chases. Before he can recover. she binds his hands and feet with bent wire coat hangers.

When this imposter wakes up she tells him. *"You will wish you're dead if anyone hurts Hiker!"* The clone cries pitifully. *"I'm only doing what I'm supposed to." "You are supposed to love me" "What's going on?"* She is astonished to realize he thinks he's telling the truth.

Once more Angela calls the same sickeningly familiar emergency number. It takes her almost a half hour to convince them to allow her to speak directly to the Director. Minutes later his secretary receives a knock at her door. Officers arrest her and she is taken to an Agency magistrate. This clone will never be seen again publicly. Upon intense interrogation the Director learns she isn't innocent as was Hiker's clone. The Director realizes how seriously these clandestine clones have penetrated the organization.

She admits to complicity with others he has under scrutiny in the kidnapping and murder of his authentic assistant. There will be a ceremony in honor of the woman she cloned at the agency. It will be said she had a heart attack induced by overwork while on a special mission. Not altogether untrue. The Director's true secretary had a weak heart; so does her clone. Both succumbed during interrogation but not by those of the same side.

That part is true; but this clones' mission wasn't for our country. Tears are shed; the Director will say, *"This marvelous person has no family but gave everything she had for her work."* Greif counselors are standing by to help those who mostly affected. However, no one really knew her well enough to truly grieve. Her work at the agency was the originals only family. As with any agency family she was bound not to discuss her work at home. So, no one knew her except the Lord.

18

MOONSHINE & MATRIMONY

While the Agency clone invasion is very real, for others in the realm of Lucien and Ralph positive things are taking place. Happiness and misery seem to happen within separate pots upon the same stove. And the mountain folk seem to be having better luck for a change. But Grace's new angel isn't sharing in their joy.

For within their little part of the hidden dimension, recovering alcoholic Roman is far from Wallow and the house on the hill. He's high and trying to stay dry up on the mountain with Grace.

Roman's cravings are rearing their nasty heads again. And as Hawk reports to Ralph, *"It ain't just beer bubbles or dandelion wine this time; old Roman has backslid sniffin on moonshine whiskey!"* Ralph rebukes him, *"Hawk! Please drop the way you are speaking."* *"If it was normal for you to talk like you think a mountaineer speaks it would be all right, but*

Angela hates pretense…Ok?"

Hawk tries to think of something bad to say but changes his mind. Instead his head goes from jet black to purple. Although his beak could easily peck a hole in Ralph, he decides not to mess with anyone whose name was once Vigilante Spirit.

"Worse, suppose Lucien directs me to watch cadavers." Hawk tries to speak without a mountain twang and decides to just keep his beak shut. But later when he tries to speak with *Dumas* he cannot make his affectation go away.

Untaxed moonshine, while desirable to many in these parts, even so it's illegal. Although he says he's accepted Jesus and is saved, Mal has decided to sell it along with mountain ginseng. He believes brewing whisky is one of those inalienable rights they all talk about. Roman reasons because Grace is his client and her sons are not, it was OK to overlook their decision to build a moonshine still. *"Just as long as nothing is attributed to Grace by the law…"*

Hunter once shot dead but recently resuscitated by a lightning bolt resists the idea of doing anything shady. Competing with his brother and having been considerably more deceased than Malcolm. He brags, *"Mal was only half dead; I was 200 proof!"*

Although Mal was critically injured and rescued by his mother he still is vulnerable to mind viruses of the kind Roman thinks up. While Wallow seems to be going well, Grace's sons Malcolm and Hunter are on a wobbly course but alive. *"Old Roman around moonshine aren't a marriage made in heaven,"* observes the ancient ghost of the mountain. *"Roman's a nice boy and my friend but keep him clear of that juice from the moonshine still."*

As usual, Mal, goes along with anyone's screwy idea regardless of consequences. His carefree nature is only slowed down because his leg will never fully recover from the injuries he received at Dumb ass's jaws. Although he's younger than Hunter his education allows Mal to overcome his older brother Hunter's more mature nature. After looking at their other employment prospects, they decide to go ahead with making moonshine.

Hardening the younger brother somewhat, there was the treachery of Buck who tried to murder Mal. Hopefully, Buck and his echo spirit are gone from this world forever. Mal convinces his naive old mother to trade some mink fur for an old moonshine still in the back of an elderly neighbors barn. He convinces her he's going to use the copper pipe to make their spring water more easily available. Because Roman helps sell this lie to Grace, he is recalled and sent back to Alcoholics Anonymous. Mal stashes the old still in a hollow near their spring. To show he is looking after Grace's best interests on the way to his AA meeting, Ralph slips a legitimate mountain product into their heads ...*Ginseng!*.

This wilderness root grows abundantly on this mountain. After vanishing beneath the earth for almost a century the brothers find it has reappeared. Lots of folks around the world believe in the rejuvenating power of ginseng, especially in Asia. Mal read about it when he was required to give a book report back in the seventh grade. His valley neighbors like it too. But they don't know where to look.

His mother insisted Mal attend school. But Hunter, who she left with their father did not receive an education. Grace took up selling small amounts of ginseng and actually earned just enough money from this and other of natures' boons for basic necessities. After raising a son below the poverty line for most of her life, Grace hasn't exactly given up on the moonshine income either. But she readily admits both moonshine and ginseng are *"the devils' tools."* She'd rather not and hopes they won't. But they will.

Sad old Roman is humiliated once again. To his credit he gets Mike and several of the other angels still stuck in the old anatomy lab to form a chapter of AA. It's one exclusively for substance abusing angels. No mortals need apply. As for refreshments at meetings for these angels, only sassafras scent and cinnamon bun essence is offered. Cherubs are in charge; they don't drink anyway but are sensitive to the problem.

After reestablishing his sobriety, Roman returns to service as Grace's guardian angel. He discovers Grace is furtively drawing off just enough moonshine to use as a means for the ginseng to float in after stuffing it into clean recycled miniature whiskey bottles. She doesn't touch the product herself. They are good for one another. Grace senses someone but chalks it off to the grace of her Lord.

Because neither Mal nor Hunter ever open the bottles they have no idea they contain whiskey. Because their customers purchase it hoping to restore vitality the few who drink the contents don't complain. The brothers have no idea their mother knows everything they do. Or that she is spiking their ginseng.

As the business picks up they deliver to Buzzardville and to some Asian restaurants on the outskirts. Only Mal delivers to Buzzardville. Because if Sheriff McPherson were to see Hunter alive he may become delusional and shoot him again. Grace warns, *"If old hornytoad McPherson sees Hunter, the old buzzard of Buzzardville could keel over dead." "That could reignite an age old feud between us on the mountain and them over there."*

As a young child, Grace remembers hearing horrific tales of past feuds and of the mourning for loved ones lost. It was a point in time no one of her generation wants to bring back. Not everything from those old days was good.

She accumulates too much cash with nowhere on the mountain to buy anything. Finally Grace visits the bank in the valley. The teller recognizes her from chapel and explains how checking accounts work. Somehow sensing the source of this newfound income is very private, her friend doesn't inquire how it was earned. However, she does caution Grace not to deposit it all at one time.

And tightlipped Grace doesn't volunteer the information. But in church, these friends smile with their eyes as Grace drops larger bills in the collection plate than ever before. But no matter how well sales go the deposits are never big enough to trigger the attention of the Feds.

Next she shops at the farm store. Everything she could ever wish for is here. Although it proudly boasts a post office and a traffic light, this mountain valley town is even smaller than Buzzardville. Grace buys seeds to disguise her ginseng enterprise. It wouldn't do to start another ginseng rush like the one that almost made it nearly disappear from her mountain.

Grace's guardian angel still approves of the enterprise. But faithful to his AA, Roman takes abstinence one day at a time. Her sons become restless and their stills are cooking mash. The scent is unmistakable and represents good financial prospects to some.

Hunter sees young women his age and has found his voice. He's no longer so shy as when he couldn't speak to strangers even to save his life. His travels now take him to people and places he didn't know existed before.

Mal has similar experiences. Routine stops bring him to where he meets young women close to his age. One young lady has made it clear she would like to go to dinner some fine evening. He discusses it with Grace and Hunter. Grace is thrilled. Although he managed to nearly get himself killed along with his friends by Hunter's dog when they attacked Hiker, he hasn't developed socially. Neither Mal nor Hunter realize the dog now called Dumas is the same retriever Hunter continually recalls. One describes a vicious rabid beast, the other a dumb and faithless duck retriever. Roman listens and is amused.

The boys meet and get to know girls up and down the mountain and the valleys in between. Finally they give up the chase and allow themselves to be caught. As everywhere, it's impossible to determine who caught whom. But when the chase ends, rings change hands and the dating is over, it is then time to ring those wedding bells. Grace informs everyone involved- *"No Shotgun Weddings are gonna happen!"*

19

Two Knot and To Not

The day has arrived for Grace's sons to marry. Little chapel windows diffuse muted light of tall new altar candles. Fresh white lilies and baby breath symbolize purity down both sides of the isle. The pews are nervous with anticipation.

Best men and bridesmaids tug at rented tuxes and new taffeta gowns anxiously awaiting the brides to be. The ring bearer lads drop their rings to no avail. Their wise moms have tied these mighty things with strings to their little boy tails.

Little did Roman think when he agreed to become Grace's guardian angel both of her sons would marry the same day. Living alone in her cabin once more, she will lose some degree of security without Mal and Hunter. Roman needs to be on guard for she is no longer in the Spring or even Fall of her lifetime. Time for her and us all keeps ticking away.

Roman could find nothing wrong with their choice of women; both wish to live a bit apart from their new mother-in-law. This means two new cabins were built upon her mountain. Luckily when Grace returned to her family land after leaving the father of her two sons she found her family forest estate and cabin intact. Her father had kept the taxes up to date and there were no loans or other incumbrances to impede her. Grace was an only child.

Her mother and father once sold a bit of timber that fortunately included some rare exotic woods. Trees whose seeds somehow managed to grow and multiply. Nothing or those is used for the cabins. Fortunately for her sons, Grace left that part of the forest green and the trees uncut and says, *"Green is your legacy."*

There are more than enough poplar and oaks nearby to produce logs in the 15 to 20 inch diameter range needed to build two cabins. Using old fashioned two-man saws, Mal and Hunter fell just enough to construct their new homes. A lot of branches are removed to create the straight logs.

Then they deftly split and stack cords of branch wood to sell for the fireplaces of the valley. For there, most trees were cleared many years ago for grazing and planting. Firewood seasons on the mountain while pork grows in the valley. And no clones will come to either.

They continue to combine their ginseng trade with firewood sales to people all throughout the valley. Grace, with subliminal encouragement from her guardian angel, managed to entice them into the same chapel where she has prayed to the Lord for so long. Grace's newest prayers will be answered if she becomes a grandmother.

On a far lower elevation than even Grace's valley chapel. a third couple might be married soon as well. If it were not for the week they decide to spend in an Ocean City condo. Clyde and his love are staying at a nice condo at 17th and the bay when she has a nostalgic impulse to visit Oriole Island. There are few licensed pilots in this area brave enough on such a windy day to hop the peninsula and splash onto the Chesapeake on pontoons.

Flush with the hot money she has from the sale of treasure Christie persuades one desperate old pilot to go along with her wishes. Soon she and Clyde are bouncing in the breeze just over this submerged Oriole whose treasures she has come to cherish. The outline of the island is etched in the water below. The pilot cautions- *"Hold on tight!"* Their plane drops like it's a rock down into the blue.

Christie opens the door wildly with the intention of making a free dive wearing just her swimsuit and nothing else. Clyde realizes her folly. Though he languished those many years as a ghost under this water, in truth poor Clyde, once more alive, can barely swim.

The notion of his time was, *"Why leave a perfectly dry ship to get wet?"* Christie is a great swimmer with and without scuba gear. She dives and within seconds she is in the cavern and has grabbed a vintage bottle of madeira. On the way out Christie steps on an unseen broken bottle. Its' razor sharp edge slices her so clean she feels no pain. Now she can't feel her blood stream out in a stream.

Clyde is barely treading water as Christy surfaces and doesn't see much until her head breaks the surface. *"I got us some desert!"* The pilot doesn't see their danger from his place in the plane. He swings open the door as Clyde tries to shove her up onto the pontoon and into the cabin.

Unfortunately, she isn't up and over quickly enough to avoid the bite of an opportunistic bull shark or two. Her bloodstream lures them. Although Clyde isn't bleeding, he's covered with hers. He puts himself between the shark and Christie. Although he is in the way of the next lunge, the bite that just wounded her is fatal. His is too.

Clyde gives up his last ounce of strength fighting to save his love. As his vision fades his body slips down into his comfortable grave under the bay; it's a perfect fit. For it is the spot that cradled his bones for many decades after he drowned here the long ago. A nearby ghost gives up the most solemn eulogy he can improvise with the simple words, *"Bones to bones Clyde."*

But this time the Grim Reaper is waiting to catch Clyde's heroic soul before it catches up with his bones. And once again Clyde will ride up to heaven in Gee's mighty ship, the El Muerte. And a second passenger is on her way with Clyde to a magnificent heavenly destination. Christie clings to him as the El Muerte reaches for a welcoming sky.

And the angels smile with ecstasy at this sight of eternal bliss. Only their pilot will fly home alone speaking to passengers who no longer are there. For time took its' toll on his mind. No memory of Clyde or Christie will be with him from this time on.

As the El Muerte once again approaches those golden gates in the sky, the traditional gatekeeper challenges- *"Everyone else gets only one shot at getting through these gates; why is this is his third!"* Gee shrugs off the question and plunges his vessel through shouting, *"Love is eternal!"*

St. Peter glares at the two lovers saying, *"Clyde, I can see you deserve a better place than your last mansion, but Christie is about at the level you were at when you charged back after her." This puts her in your old place and you at one considerably higher." "Or, you both can share your same old place." "What's it going to be?"*

Although Christie is still aghast at just how fast she went from being alive on earth to a soul in heaven she's determined Clyde isn't going to suffer because of her. *"I'm ready to go to hell rather than have Clyde lose out in any way."* The gatekeeper comforts her soul. Then gives Gee two passes to an even higher celestial home.

Back in Grace's world, nuptials aren't as complicated for the couples back in the valley. Grace's sons wait at the altar for their new brides to walk down the aisle. Malcolm and Hunter are nervously pacing up and down in their baggy rented tuxedo jackets for their first time ever. While the jackets are baggy, the trousers are tight and itch. Standing, waiting, itching, but they can't scratch. So they each do a little dance and the brides trip down the aisle. The guests on the grooms side of the chapel think it's a custom and soon all of them are dancing in their pews. Grace feints.

Their brides arrive; the procession down to the altar is elegant. A delightful aspect of this wedding is no one spoils this ceremony, thanks to Grace's guardian angel. Roman stands guard atop the steeple brandishing a flaming sword as Hawk circles directly overhead screaming at any and all demons...even Satan to stay away. Roman roars *"I'm an angry recovering alcoholic who has no one. And nothing to lose. I will send all of you to hell in a billion pieces if you try anything!"* None dares challenge the mighty Roman with withdrawal shakes, least of all the demons.

20

CLONES

He starts by stating the high level of classification of the discussion to follow. Then an individual carrying a black box with a scanning probe enters the room. He walks behind each person and nods in affirmation of their natural state of being. Only one seems to require a longer scan. He explains his neck is infused with an appliance brought about by an explosion in a foreign land. The Director thanks him for his service.

After the technician leaves the door is secured. The Director speaks- *"Not since the Greeks deceived the Trojans has any insertion been so diabolical as the one you have endured." "Of course there has been espionage and spies; that's to be expected, but this was in an entire new class of deception." "In each case, except my own, the spy did not know it wasn't real." "Fortunately, the clone who was supposed to be me, came apart and we learned much from the device implanted inside."* An exhaling of breath is heard as the group emits a sigh of relief.

The Director continues- *"We think we have all of the surviving clones in our stockade." "And we have listened to their conversations." "It is obvious they are very confused; they think it's all a big mistake." "From the earliest scientific experiments back when a sheep named Dolly was duplicated, clones have had a relatively short lifespan." "We are seeing signs of this in the group we collected as well." "Therefore it is also logical to believe new clones will arrive to replace those previously dispatched as replacements." "You must be constantly vigilant and report anything and everything suspicious."*

"Are there any questions?" The group is too stunned to ask anything. *"After a brief lunch, we are going by bus to the compound where we will let each of you interrogate your double from behind a one way glass." "We don't want them to realize who you are." "Hopefully, their answers will provide some insight concerning the origins of the intelligence sources*

used to construct their minds." "By the way, at lunch follow your normal dietary preference; eat nothing you wouldn't ordinarily consume." "We want to learn if they eat the same as you."

The group thoughtfully selected their lunches in the Agency cafeteria trying to remember their preferences. Because people often eat without thinking of what it is they're putting in their mouths, looks of consternation gave way to confusion in a number of cases. But, finally everyone sits down and are chopping away at what they think is their normal diet.

The Director stands up facing his subordinates back in the blue military bus. *"Ask questions that deal with events further back in time than when you came to the Agency." "Then, move to about the time you started with us, followed by even more recent events." "As most of you are analysts, you shouldn't have any trouble knowing what to ask."*

Four guards armed with automatic weapons check out the bus exterior with mirrors and other devices. Then the driver and another climbed on board. He walks down the aisle comparing the photos on the badges with the wearers. Perhaps everyone onboard realized at the same moment the futility of the comparison of photographs where clones are involved. But no one dared say a word. Reading their minds, the Director simply rolls his eyes.

The group files in through the rear doors of the interrogation facility and are seated. Their clones arrive next and file obediently into their cafeteria area. The Director provides each of his men a folder and a device to record their impersonator. Casually the impersonators finish lunch and are gently escorted to an area where each clone can be observed but cannot see its' subject.

Questions and answers are asked and recorded. *"Where did you attend school?"* *"Who did you take to the prom?"* And so on. Soon the clones are back in their rooms. And the interrogators return to their bus. They started to compare notes on the bus, but the Director told them to save everything until they got back to the Agency where their observations can be properly analyzed. Hiker mouth is shut tight while his mind races all of the way back.

Once again they are in the room where they started. The Director opened with a basic question, *"How far back in time did your clones' memory of you go?"* In every case they answered, *"Just since I came with the Agency."* The next question, *"How did your clones' diet compare with yours?"* The answers were mixed until they realized that two included dietary restrictions just imposed only weeks ago by the Agency medical officer during routine physicals.

The Director diffused the ensuing anger against the doctor by pointing out that the doctors' records were probably hacked. *"The doctor may be completely innocent."* The irony of where they were and the idea their own records were hacked first strikes one funny. Then others, and finally the Director. As a group they scream laughing until one rolls on the floor and has to be removed.

"That's all for today, you will be returned to your own duty section parking lots." Looking at Hiker, he added the

assurance the drivers have all been verified not to be clones. And the perfunctory, *"Thank you all for taking time from your vital duties to be here."* And Hiker thinks to himself, "As though we had a choice."

The following month the Director calls another meeting. A different group has been selected. This is a meeting to provide an update on the clone situation. Those invited today are only Agency employees whose lives have been most affected by counterfeits bearing their images. When the small room is full he signals for the doors to be sealed. His image fades from the screen. The audience is anesthetized. After several minutes, fans clear the air and security reenters with litters.

He learned each original person has been murdered and was replaced by the clones in attendance. However, these will be held and studied. Their nature is such the process of becoming what they are decimates their longevity. They will replace those previously imprisoned who have now died. This process will repeat once every quarter until no more clones arrive. The system will work.

Ralph and Lucien split up for the day. Ralph stays with his charge as guardian angel. Lucien heads back to the detention center. She wants to learn as much as possible about these humanoids.

Most of all she wants to know why they have targeted people she knows. Yet she realizes through his work Hiker has made himself a target for human demons of all stripes. If so, there are limits to her power. But, if there are demons of the dimension hidden from the eyes of human beings then angels become their defense. For defense against demonic forces is the business of angels.

She hovers over the site. The only guardian angels present are for the guards. None of the prisoners have one. She sidles up to a guards' angel. She jokes in the idiom of the area, *"Hey babe!" "What's happenin'?"* Her bored counterpart matches he tone with- *"Nonthin' mama, what's happenin with you?"* In her normal more businesslike voice Lucien asks,

"What's with them?" "Are they dangerous?" The angel nods, *"They are just as dangerous as the human beings who programed them...no more, no less."*

The guardian angel of the detention guard must be careful not to tell Lucien anything that could put her own charge at a disadvantage. Both know this, but they also can sense the inherent danger of these clones as well. Who knows what they've been programmed to do or who to murder? The guards' angel volunteers the location of a testing laboratory. It is in a room far beneath them. It's where the device from a dead clone is studied...in fact the Director clone.

When the Director clone wiped out with Hiker in the corvette back in the tunnel, that clone was mostly destroyed. But a black device was found implanted at the base of the skull. The guards' angel focuses Lucien's attention at the ceilings of the detention center and even the awnings over the exercise area. The insulated coverings present a major obstacle to any signals coming or going. The angel tells Lucien, *"These clone people are withering fast... I suspect they are suffering*

from sensory deprivation and something else I can't define."
"But there is little doubt more of these will soon die." "They
do what the guards tell them, but do not talk to guards or even
among themselves." "And frankly, they don't seem to know
much of anything beyond basic skills." "They are directed one
piece at a time." "It's obviously primitive."

Lucien thanks the guard and sets off for the underground testing center. Finding anything here is nearly impossible though. The Agency is like a maze; there are endless corridors leading to nowhere. She is nearly ready to give up when she detects a very faint signal pulse coming from deep beneath the hall she's in.

Fortunately, for her pursuit, the Agency has no sensors tuned to angel. She simply follows the signal until its's strength increases to a point where she reaches the testing room. There are no clones; just a scientist and a technician and the bar retrieved from the dead clone.

The scientist explains to her assistant, *"Their communications bars are identical." "They seem to have two modes." "One is a low long distance receiver." "The other very high frequency mode is a transmitter." "That means someone, or something relatively nearby is capable of communicating with this device." "This is how the clones receive instructions and report back to whoever is running their show."*

"There's nothing high tech about these duplex transmissions." "We must continually monitor these signals." "They are capable of receiving of sending both which amounts to odd communication." "It's probable the low frequency end of this is just for receiving orders." "Who knows? Maybe the internet may also be involved; we need to keep an open mind to any possibility."

Lucien is ten steps ahead of them. She is out of the room and is following the higher frequency. She follows a path of white lights leading to a tall nearby building. It's coming from a hotel. One where one room serves as a clandestine communications hub for each different clone series. The first one's for the Director clones. But, this one hasn't transmitted since the Director clone crashed because its' replacement hasn't arrived. There are no friendly angels here to question. So, Angela doesn't know where or when the next clone will arrive.

There are three human occupiers in the hotel room; none are clones. Yet not one of the three has a guardian angel either. Lucien summons Ralph. Her husband's a good angel with a wicked hacker past. Ralph very stealthily turns on the transmitter and jacks up the signal strength making it immediately visible to those in the Agency testing lab. In fact the device starts vibrating and overheats, all of which is recorded. The signal is easily traced by the monitors.

Shortly the door to the room swings open. Three enemy agents are arrested and charged with operating a powerful transmitter without an FCC license. They will be held without bail under rules designed in the wake of 911. They also will be interrogated in a much more intensive manner than were clones earlier.

There is no doubt they are enemy agents of someone…but for who? Although subjected to the most intense questioning allowed by law they do not know who they work for even while admitting the kidnapping and murder of the Director's assistant. For these are hired mercenaries. Other rooms along this floor are raided with similar outcomes.

Although the captive clones are treated well, they continue dying after several months in captivity. They stop eating and even though they are force fed with tubes they simply fade. Autopsies reveal something shocking. Their bodies are rejecting parts transplanted. When the medical officer reports findings to the Director's staff at their weekly meeting, he advises that any future clones should be treated with immune suppression drugs. And he dolefully admits the strong possibility that in turn will leave them subject to infection. The Director is unsympathetic.

Newly arriving clones are easily captured due to the interrogations of the first wave. They all are dropped off at a small island at the mouth of the Magothy River where a local fisherman transfers them to shore. However, the local fisherman is also a clone. The message transmitted to him on the low frequency when a transfer is needed is intercepted and as soon as he drops off his passengers they are arrested. He is tolerated. Because, how else would the Agency know?

Strangely, clones are short lived. Their immune systems were intentionally comprised by medication when the two components of their beings were grafted. Otherwise rejection will kill them even quicker. Without some protection, they are like the worlds' indigenous populations when they came in contact with others who had developed immunities.

As their communications network unravels, more clones throughout the world are captured. The new problem is to find past transfers to uncover damage to the world at their hands. Thanks to a large body of broad spectrum recordings within the Agency, the FBI and other federal bodies are able to reverse engineer known past incursions. As this is being written, more arrests are underway. Yet they won't stop coming.

Although this wholesale production of cloned spies keeps Hiker's section and others busy, this is also of concern to the angels to the extent their human charges are endangered. And that becomes less and less. Lucien and Ralph consider it a pastime to learn the source of clones. To satisfy their curiosity they will follow the trail back to the source.

21

FINALITY

"What did it all amount to?" she asks. *"Would you do it all over if you had a choice?"* *"No!"* he jokes. *"I didn't think so."* *"Not that I had a choice."* he fires back. *"But you had a choice; are you sorry?"* she demands to know. *"No, I did the best I could with very little."* He exaggerates submissively. *"Are you sorry you married me?"* *"Of course not; I love you!"*

Gee overhears them and thinks, *"So this is the way of lovers within every dimension."* Ralph and Lucien understand he's been eavesdropping again as usual and passionately embrace without thinking another word out loud. Love sparring conversations like this are rare for Ralph and Lucien.

That is because they are workaholics. Each day they hover over each venue they try to improve assessing each one. They hover now over Wallow. Right away Lucien sees the progress. *"Angela eventually will see a return on her investment if not here, up there in heaven."*

Lizard Alley's ashes and debris from the fire have been scraped up. It was replaced by an upscale condo. No vestige of its' previous decrepit state remains. Lucien is incredibly pleased, *"Thanks to Gee, not a demonic ghost remains."* He explains, *"Demons try to pop back up once in a while but that's just natural everywhere."* He agrees. *"When they're thrown out of one haunt they just gravitate to another."*

Lucien isn't as happy about the way things have gone back at the house with Angela and Hiker. *"His work puts them both in jeopardy!"* Ralph defends his charge, *"It isn't his fault; Hiker had no way of knowing they were in the sights of both demons and international terrorists when he took the job at the Agency."*. He shrugs, *"It's just life!"* Lucien nags happily. *"Ours is not JUST LIFE; remember we aren't really alive in the way of mortals."*

In a more appeasing tone, she rationalizes *"At least we made amends to that old cruise ship captain you once left in* nothing but a lady's bra and panties at his captains' table.'' Ralph retorts, *"After the old captain was discharged from the cruise line I put him in charge of the new Wallow casino."* *"You know I did that!"*

Lucien laughs, *"Yeah! And do you realize he wanted to make the card counters and everyone else who tries to cheat the casino walk the plank over the tiger cage at our new zoo?"* Lucien deeply explores Ralph's sense of right and wrong, *"Do you still really believe he deserved everything you did to him?"* *"... just because the cruise line temporarily misplaced all of the passenger luggage?"*

Lucien rubs it in- *"You had him holding captains table at a 4,000 passenger cruise ship in nothing but a ladies bra and panties!"* *"After doing that, how was he supposed to run a tight ship?"* Ralph snickers, *"In pink tights?"* Lucien chokes laughing.

Realizing he's on thin ice with her, sheepishly he admits, *"OK, so I was too hard on the old guy."* She asks- *"So, what do we do with any of those cheaters who he actually makes walk the plank and who are mauled or killed?"* He shrugs and

changes the subject, *"I'm bored, let's go on a cruise..."*

22

HONEYMOON

They both know, the disgruntled old cruise captain isn't a swashbuckler, even if he makes noises like one. He says, *"Let's see if Roman will cover for us while we're gone."* There is no privacy in the dimension of angels and demons, so everyone hears their comment including Roman who presently is completely sober and has been for ten days and counting.

Roman has finally accepted rejection by Lucien. Moreover, he's developed a grudging respect for the accomplishments and finishing tweaks of Ralph after he became an angel. Worse yet, he's bored with being Grace's guardian angel because she never gets in trouble. Now that Mal and Hunter are off on their own she's more perfect than even he. Her demons are vanquished, and the devil has given up on tempting her.

They accept Roman's help to watch over the house and its' inhabitants as well as Grace and hers. Ralph's transition from Vigilante Spirit to angel was so exhausting there wasn't time for their honeymoon. Their timing may sound strange to cruise novices. They will take a cruise during a hurricane in the Atlantic, one that is designed to move the cruise ship to a new seasonal area.

Lucien explains, *"These are called repositioning cruises and attract a more adventuresome group."* She adds- *"And, angels don't catch people viruses."* Dumas snorts, *"I'll bet dogs catch viruses from people and angels!"* Hawk moans, *"I hope I can't catch avian germs."*

Nearly every ship has its' share of angels and demons. So, much so that cruise ships often have chaplains. Ralph and Lucien are supposedly onboard the big ship to recover their mental stamina as well as to honeymoon. The myriad of labors and emergencies they have dealt with during the short time they have been married would have tried the patience of saints.

Angela reminds him, *"We're just here for the ride...no vigilante shenanigans this time..."* Ralph just grins.

He looks around. *"This ship is considerably larger than the Dawns Early Light, the one I was on when you dropped down out of the sky,"* Looking out over the expanse of the grey blue Atlantic only a few gulls can be seen sailing over the waves. When they fly over the ship, they hover just above unoccupied deck chairs. The passengers stare out over a seemingly limitless blue sea. Gulls scream when they find popcorn left from the open deck movies of the night before.

A furious hurricane twists and spins somewhere out there but the skill of the ships' captain steers them far away from that chaotic storm. But each morning the captain announces a new mysterious destination well off of the planned route. He tags their voyage for the day, *"a mystery cruise."*

For the first few days everything seems idyllic and rewarding. Because through selective memory erasures and fine negotiation the old Captain is back at sea with a different cruise line. Nut with an abnormal interest in the ships' casino though. Occasionally in nightmares he screams, *"Keelhaul!";* *keelhaul!, keelhaul!"* He's not alone. The cruise director whose bra and panties he appropriated when he captained The Dawns Early Light and he now travel together in one cabin. It's said she wears the pants of the two.

The idea of hauling anyone from one side of the barnacle ridden hull to the other is a barbaric vestige of olden times on the sea. But, it's history has seeped into the captain's mind. Lucien just smiles and tells Ralph, *"If he only knew, he would keelhaul you."* *"...If he only could get his hands on you for all of the trouble you caused him."* Ralph quips, *"...but he can't."*

Ralph tries to change the subject, *"I wonder how the devil feels down in his sewer beneath the pits of hell?"* She says, *"Don't ask Gee; having to put Satan down there back when that all came down took all of his resolve."* *"I won't."*

"Do you think Hiker will ever get over the fact he was cloned?" No, and that joker at the agency who took his tissue sample won't either." The Director has him languishing down

in the detention center along with those other phonies." "There are so many clones in there they could start their own agency." He adds. *"For at least a week."* Ralph and Lucien hope to discover the source of the clones. This cruise isn't just for their honeymoon or pleasure.

They arrive at Kings' Wharf in Bermuda and stay just long enough to feel a sample of the Caribbean atmosphere. Then they float over the rail onto a ship tied up just behind the one they've been on. This one is setting course for Southampton in the England. As usual they settle in a quiet corner where they can watch the passengers. There is nothing now for an angel to do. So they just enjoy one another and their honeymoon.

Once the ship docks at Southampton, they take a quick trip into London. There they find a minor problem. It seems the royal corgi's have slipped the queen's keepers and have taken to the streets like common pooches. One tries to steal a plate of fish and chips from a pub on the west end but isn't high enough off of the ground to reach its' prize. Lucien inspires a patron to hoist it up. The dog's chow down fish and chips like hogs.

They bolt down the chips, gobbles the fish, and can't figure out what to do with mushy peas. A corgi looks at a patron wondering, *"Why in the world do you like mushy peas?" "We just don't get it!"* So, it does just that; it gets down. The barkeep takes note and the dogs are scooted back outside without the usual royal pomp and ceremony. Without her majesty, a dog is just a dog.

Black helmeted angels in bobbies' uniforms usher both corgis back to Buckingham Palace. They turn down their normal food; the Queen frets they may be ill. But the stench of stale ale on their doggy breath gives them away. The Queen is no fool; for her highness has tipped a few pints of her own in tune with times long past.

Her majesty mutters to herself, *"What can I dress as today that will fool everyone?" "I could really use a pint!"* Well, not altogether quite to herself, a servant notifies Scotland

Yard, *"She's at it again." "This time her majesty is dressed as a nun." "She's taking a pint at Paddy McBunn's"*

The royalty has its' own guardian angels and need no help from American angels. Ralph and Lucien follow the tourists back to Southampton. Their ship is heading for ports unknown to avoid the storm. This one makes it to Figo a charming port in Spain. And, here the honeymooners feel a touch of heaven. Spain's' angels hospitably welcome Lucien and Ralph. The streets are lined with ghosts who have heard of Ralph and are happy to welcome Lucien.

Lucien takes the opportunity to ask whether anyone has seen any evidence of clones in this area. The question takes the Spanish by surprise. They have not but are very curious. *"Why, why, why?"* they ask. She tells of their mischief in detail. All that occurred back in Maryland. Their Spanish counterparts promise to exchange any information about clones and ask Ralph and Lucien to reciprocate as well. But, no one knows for sure if a clone has a soul.

And some young Spanish angels much like their human counterparts do flirt. Lucien stops one from making eyes at Ralph with a flip of her eyes. *"There was once a demon, she sighs."* This dark eyed beauty smiles and flows off saying something Ralph can't understand and which Lucien refuses to interpret.

Leaving the lovelies and beauty of Spain, they return to the ship after it departs by gliding over the dock and flowing in its' wake out to sea. They rarely make to the ship on time but never are they left behind.

Ralph pesters her to know what was said, she lies, *"She said you are gordo and yucky."* Gullible Ralph looks at himself saying, *"Even I know gordo means fat!" "Let's go to the ships' gym and workout."*

Even so, thinking back to the conversation, he doesn't remember hearing the word "gordo." Lucien makes a mental note to send Roman to this beautiful place. Here that frustrated angel may find love.

As the mortals have breakfast on the ship, the captain announces another change in course. *"To avoid the bad weather further north Atlantic the ship will detour to the Azores."* Within a day their ship finds its' way to charming Ponta Delgada, an Atlantic Portuguese port.

The city's inhabitants are so courteous the angels see little necessity for traffic lights. These drivers courteously stop and take turns at some of the busiest intersections. Just offshore the ocean is so clean and blue, bathers and boats share space peacefully. And their so-called *regional wines* are in complete harmony with the pulse of the island. Both beat sweetly and gently.

As Lucien and Ralph flow into a stone piazza in front of the cathedral an island angel beckons. He tells them of very strange things going on not far from where they hover. Hidden within a charming little village is a devilish endeavor almost in plain sight. But almost means most of it is hidden from mortal eyes, but not the eyes of angels.

Beneath modest white cottages for all to see, science has run amuck. People who never went in are coming out. This lone sentry is alone in this small village and wonders why this is happening. He states, *"Nearly all who were born in our beautiful Azores have guardian angels; none of these have even one."* *"How can this be?"*

Once Juan understands clones are showing up on the U.S. east coast, the three angels realize they have been working on the same puzzle from opposite sides of the ocean. They agree the problem is not one for mere angels to solve. *"How often does the grim reaper stop by, asks Ralph."* The angel replies, *"Not so often because our mortals pray often, sleep well and live nearly forever."*

Word travels faster than the speed of light within the dimension of good angels and even some not so good. The ultimate solution of human clones is a puzzle only the Almighty can solve. It is obvious to the three angels those leaving this place are not normal clones. They are a combination of a grown individual with another persons' DNA superimposed. The sentry angel's orders are just to watch and report.

Ralph and Lucien will resume their cruise as though nothing has happened. And in a week or so they will return to their duties in the big house on the hill. They are determined to continue their honeymoon. And believe they have discovered enough about clones to develop a position on the subject when they get back. But it is obvious to both others in their dimension must be aware of this bizarre place. For nothing escapes their sight. It must be a matter of nations outside of our purview.

Back at the house on the hill, Angela has given birth to twins, a boy and girl. Hiker and Angela are happy with their twins. Dumas believes he only exists to protect them all. Roman stops by once in awhile to see them. He gradually has come to accept Hiker although when he lived here he was in a haze much of the time. The newborn twins will each have a dedicated guardian angel if Lucien has anything to say about it.

A quick audit of the cadavers of an old anatomy lab in Baltimore finds some of these folks have been either laid to rest or cremated. Each earthly burial or cremation enables a guardian angel to become available. But Lucien will have none of some of Mike's old beer bubble sops. She waits for just the right angel for Angela's *"little darlings."* No one dares contradict Lucien on this matter, nor about much else.

Wallow is finally producing a slight profit for Angela after a delay too long for any normal investor. Ralph is becoming restless. He longs to become involved with direct intervention against the cowards of the mortal world. But, leaving Lucien is beyond the pale; he loves her, and she loves him as much.

He volunteers to back up the overworked guardian angels of a harried police force. Although each cop has a guardian angel, they welcome a volunteer. After several interventions, his need to see justice is fulfilled. According to the chief. *"Ralph's just too rough!"*

One particular incident involved a domestic call in West Baltimore. A woman's husband was beating her. When the policeman got there he pulled the drunken husband to the floor and tried to handcuff him. For reasons only she knows, the battered wife hit him over the head with their old style wall phone.. Before she could hit him a second time, Ralph blurred her vision and she bashed in her kneecap instead. Two ended the day in jail; the heroic policeman must live on with his pain.

The SLUGS and thugs of Wallow have all been sanitized, isolated, or banished. Criminals have found other places easier. And as usual follow the low hanging fruit. Buzzardville mourns the late Sheriff McPherson. A concrete monument has been erected to remind Buzzardvillains of his loyalty and service.

Just before being run out of town on a rail, after being tarred and feathered, the newspaper editor made an irreverent error citing an old ditty, *"They laid him in the ground boys; they laid him in the ground boys... one less here and one more there they laid him in the ground..."* But, as with others, the sheriffs' earthly deeds and misdeeds leave him in limbo.

Sheriff McPherson's ghost will haunt the old chapel cemetery for many years to come. When the old gravedigger went to bury him, the easiest place to dig was the very spot his victim, Hunter once was lain.

The gravedigger doesn't remember much until he comes across a bottle he had tossed in after burying Hunter. He gives up drinking forever. And decides, *"I think I'll apply for a job as his replacement tomorrow."* Apply he might but the good folks of Buzzardville know him only too well. And as one points out- *"If we make him sheriff, who are we going to get to pick up the roadkill?"* Not much ever changes in Buzzardville. No one likes strangers and no one ever forgives or forgets. And that's the damned charm of the place they call Buzzardville town.

As for Ralph and Lucien and their charges, everything is fine. As new clones sent to create problems for the world are dropping before their time. Lucien knows the problem has passed. But if the past is an indication of things to come within the hidden dimension, one realizes the absolute best angels and the most horrible demons will remain locked in their perpetual battle for the souls of all mortal forever.